As a child, Marilyn Halvorson loved to read books about the Wild West and life on a ranch. When she was just twelve, she received a typewriter for Christmas and began to write stories. Today she is the author of several award-winning books for young adults, all set in Western Canada, including *Dare, Brothers and Strangers, Stranger on the Run*, and *Cowboys Don't Cry*, which won the Clarke Irwin–Alberta Culture Writing for Youth Competition in 1983 and was made into a popular television movie.

A keen observer of relationships, Ms. Halvorson draws heavily on her experiences as a teacher and rancher for ideas.

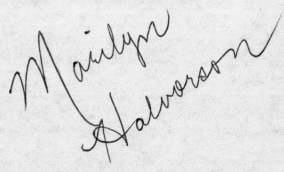

MARILYN HALVORSON

BUT COWS CAN'T FLY
AND OTHER STORIES

A JUNIOR GEMINI BOOK

Published in 1993 by
Stoddart Publishing Co. Limited
34 Lesmill Road
Toronto, Canada
M3B 2T6
(416) 445-3333

Canadian Cataloguing in Publication Data

Halvorson, Marilyn, 1948–
But cows can't fly: and other stories

"Junior Gemini"
ISBN 0-7736-7403-9

I. Title.

PS8565.A46B8 1993   jC813'.54   C93-094466-6
PZ7.H35Bu 1993

Cover design: Brant Cowie/ArtPlus
Typesetting: Tony Gordon Ltd.
Printed and bound in the United States of America

Note regarding the story "Mr. Who?": Carol Kelly
is a real person and the Medicine River Wildlife
Rehabilitation Centre is a real place. Readers
interested in finding out more about helping
injured wildlife are invited to contact her at the
Medicine River Wildlife Rehabilitation Centre,
Box 115, Spruceview, Alberta T0M 1V0.

Stoddart Publishing gratefully acknowledges the
support of the Canada Council, the Ontario
Ministry of Culture, Tourism, and Recreation,
Ontario Arts Council, and Ontario Publishing
Centre in the development of writing and
publishing in Canada.

Contents

THE TREE COW

The wind woke Jodie McCrimmon on her second night at Grandma and Grandpa's ranch. It howled and tore at the window like a wild animal trying to get in. It scared Jodie. Twice she jumped out of bed and started toward Grandma and Grandpa's bedroom. But twice Jodie made herself get back into bed. She was ten years old now and starting her year here on the ranch. No old wind was going to make a scaredy-cat crybaby out of her. She watched the glowing numbers on the clock radio beside the bed. The radio was her friend. Once, with the volume very

1

low, she turned it on just to make sure the rest of the world was still out there. It was. The disc jockey's voice was warm and happy. He wasn't afraid of the wind. Slowly, Jodie closed her eyes . . .

When she opened them again the window was a square of pale daylight. Down the hall the kitchen light shone bright and welcoming. Jodie jumped into her warm red bathrobe and hurried to the kitchen.

Grandpa's blue eyes twinkled at her over the top of a steaming cup of coffee. "Well, Jodie-kid, it's about time you were up! How am I going to get those cows fed if you don't help me?"

"Do we have to feed the cows in a blizzard, Grandpa?"

Grandpa's eyes looked puzzled. "What blizzard, Jodie? It's melting out there today."

It was Jodie's turn to be puzzled. "Melting? But when we looked at the thermometer at bedtime it was below zero, and didn't you hear the wind last night?"

Before Grandpa could answer, the door opened and Grandma came in from feeding the barn cats. "Whew!" she said, pulling off her jacket, "that ol' chinook sure did re-arrange the woods last night."

Now Jodie was *really* confused. "Who's Ol' Chinook?"

It was Grandpa that answered, the corner of his eyes crinkly with little laugh lines. "Ol' Chinook is who you heard howling last night, Jodie-kid. Look out the window and you'll see what he's done."

Jodie pulled back the curtain and looked out into the mud-puddled barnyard. "Grandpa!" she whispered, wide-eyed, "where's the snow?"

"Well," Grandpa began, reaching out to circle Jodie's shoulders with a big, warm hug, "that fire-breathing dragon, Ol' Chinook, up and melted it clean away!"

Grandma just shook her head. "Harold! For goodness' sake, you'll have poor Jodie so confused she won't know what to believe about Alberta. The truth is, Jodie, that the chinook is a wind that comes across the mountains from B.C. It starts out full of moisture from the Pacific Ocean but by the time it climbs above the Rockies it loses all its moisture and comes here to the foothills warm and dry. It can raise winter temperatures from thirty below to above freezing in just a few hours."

Jodie thought that over. "Wow," she said at last, "Ol' Chinook sure must be full of hot air!"

"You can say that again," Grandpa said with a chuckle. "Now hurry up and eat your breakfast. We've got work to do."

Twenty minutes later Jodie and Grandpa were bouncing along the pasture trail in the beat-up old farm truck. Jodie sat turned around in the seat watching the huge bale of sweet green hay unrolling from the bale handler on the back of the truck just like a giant roll of paper towels.

Big fat red-and-white cows galloped playfully along behind, stopping now and then to grab a bite of hay, then rushing to catch up in case they'd missed a better bite. All of a sudden Grandpa slammed on the brakes. Jodie turned to see what was wrong. Right across the trail in front of them lay a giant, broken-off spruce tree.

"What happened to the tree, Grandpa?"

"That's some of Ol' Chinook's handi-work, Jodie. Look out there in the woods and you'll see lots more of it."

Jodie's eyes followed Grandpa's pointing finger. Here and there all through the thick spruce woods where the cows bedded down in the winter were more broken trees. Some were broken near the bottom like the big one across the trail. Others were like snaggly witches' teeth. Their trunks were still standing but their bushy green tops had been snapped off and tossed to the ground.

"Wow! And I thought it was scarey in *my* bedroom last night. Bet the cows were scared out here."

Grandpa smiled. "Cows live with all kinds of weather all their lives. I think they pretty much learn to take it all in their stride."

Jodie shook her head thoughtfully. "You know, Grandpa, it sure is nice to have Ol' Chinook bring us summer in January, but I don't know if that makes it worthwhile having him around. He sure does play rough."

That afternoon Grandma and Grandpa and Jodie all had dentists' appointments in

Calgary, so nobody thought much more about chinooks for the rest of the day. The next day school started again after Christmas holidays. It was Jodie's first day in her new school and she was a little bit nervous.

And she missed her mom and dad a little, too. They were away in Africa travelling and doing field research on endangered animals. They would be gone for a whole year. It seemed such a long time. But Jodie reminded herself that they'd promised to write lots of letters about their adventures. And she would write to them, too, about all her adventures on the ranch with Grandma and Grandpa and all the animals there.

Grandma drove her to town and took her to meet the principal and her new teacher. They were nice, but Jodie still felt kind of scared as Grandma turned to leave. Grandma bent low to whisper in her ear. "Don't tell Grandpa I told you this, 'cause it's supposed to be a surprise, but he's getting something very special for you today."

Jodie opened her mouth to ask questions, but Grandma just put a finger to her lips, winked, and disappeared out the door.

The day flew by. The kids in Jodie's class were friendly. They were really impressed when she could already do the kind of math problems they were just learning. On the way home on the bus, a boy named Eric, who lived just down the road from Jodie, asked if she'd like to go riding sometime.

"I'd really like to go, Eric, but I don't have a horse," Jodie said.

Eric looked disappointed. "Aw, that's too bad. Well, maybe you can borrow my sister's horse sometime if she's not feeling too ornery. My sister, I mean. Her horse is a lot easier to get along with than she is."

Jodie giggled. "Thanks for asking, Eric. Maybe something will work out." The bus ground to a stop at the end of the lane and Jodie jumped out. She ran all the way to the house, her mind on the surprise. She flung open the back door and dumped her books on the table.

"Grandma! Grandpa! I'm home!" she called. Her voice echoed hollowly through the dim, empty house. A cold stab of loneliness and disappointment went through her. Some surprise! No one was even home.

Then she glanced out the window and saw the light on in the barn. She raced out of the house and went charging into the barn. "Grandma! Grandpa!" she yelled.

Suddenly Grandpa stepped out of the shadows. "Hush, Jodie-kid, you're going to spook Lady."

"Who's Lady?"

Then Grandma stepped out of the shadows. She was holding a rope. On the other end of the rope was a halter, and wearing the halter was a beautiful little black horse with a white blaze on its face. "This," Grandma said proudly, "is Lady. And she's your new horse."

Jodie just stood there and stared. "*My* horse?" she whispered.

"Is there an echo in here?" Grandpa teased as Grandma held out the halter rope to Jodie.

"Oh Grandma, Grandpa! Thank you!" Jodie threw her arms around Lady's neck, breathing in the rich, clean horse smell of her thick, black mane. "Can I take her out for a ride right now? Please? Please?"

Grandpa hesitated. "Well, I don't know about that. It's getting late . . ."

Grandma gave Grandpa a nudge. "Oh come on, Harold, don't be a stick-in-the-mud. You saw how well Jodie can ride back at the stable in Vancouver where she took lessons. Let her go for a few minutes."

Grandpa gave in. "Well, okay. But just out in the close cow pasture, and you get back here before dark."

"You bet, Grandpa!"

Jodie led Lady outside, checked that the cinch on the saddle was tight, and climbed on. Grandpa opened the pasture gate and Lady set off obediently up the trail, behaving just the way her name said she would.

Jodie still couldn't believe that Lady was hers. It was all so wonderful. She rode past the cows who were just finishing up the last of the day's hay. "Look, cows. This is my new horse. You'd better be nice to her 'cause she's a real Lady!" Lady bobbed her head up and down as if she was agreeing with that. Jodie giggled and reined Lady off the main trail. "Come on, Lady. Let's go home through the woods and count how many trees Ol' Chinook knocked down."

Jodie was in such a good mood she even talked to the trees. "Sorry to see you've broken your trunk, Mr. Spruce. Just lie still and it won't hurt. Oh, Mrs. Poplar, your branch has blown away and got tangled in Mr. Pine's hair. He'll have to see if he can sew it back on for you with his needles!" Lady gave a loud, disdainful snort. Jodie had to agree. That was a pretty weak joke.

For a while she rode in silence. The only sound was the soft thud of Lady's hooves on the forest floor. That was why she heard it so clearly when the huge fallen spruce tree spoke to her. Instantly, she pulled Lady to a stop and sat frozen in the saddle staring at the bushy tree that lay nearby. It looked just like a dozen other fallen trees she had seen. But she knew for a fact that it *had* spoken. It had said, quite distinctly, "Moo."

"Lady," Jodie whispered, "tell me you heard that tree."

But Lady just tossed her head and refused to comment. Jodie glanced around the darkening forest. The friendly trees were looking spookier every second. She wouldn't have been surprised if that crooked poplar had suddenly hissed like a giant cobra or the tall skinny spruce howled like a hungry wolf. But none of the trees made a sound. Except for the big, bushy, fallen spruce. Quite loudly, it said "Moo!" again.

"Okay, that does it!" Jodie said, jumping off her horse to bend down for a closer look. "Either there's a cow under that tree or I really am losin' it!" She pulled back a couple of branches and peered into the shadowy depths of the fallen tree. There, peering right back out at her was a white face and two big worried cow eyes.

Jodie felt her own eyes getting just about as big as the cow's. "Hang on there, old girl!" she called, already pulling herself back into Lady's saddle. "I'll be back to rescue you!" She kicked Lady into a gallop and headed for home.

Grandpa and Grandma heard the hoof-beats long before they saw Jodie. They were both waiting by the barnyard gate looking angry and worried. "Now you listen here, Jodie," Grandma began, "if I'd known you didn't have any more sense than to go charging through the woods at that speed I'd have never let you go . . ."

"But Grandma," Jodie interrupted breathlessly, "there's a cow out there . . ."

"By last count there were sixty-three cows out there and that still doesn't give you any excuse to . . ."

Jodie took a deep breath and tried again. "No, Grandpa, you don't understand. There's a cow out there trapped under a fallen tree!"

The anger drained out of Grandpa's face, and a look of sadness took its place. "You mean she's dead," he said, sounding discouraged and tired.

"No! No, Grandpa! She's very much alive. She called to me for help as I rode by!"

Grandpa and Grandma exchanged glances. "I suppose she's hurt too bad to save," Grandpa said softly.

Grandma sighed. "Most likely, Harold, but we'll have to see what we can do. Put her out of her misery at least. I'll go get the rifle out of the house while you get the chain saw so we can saw the tree off and have a look."

By the time Grandma and Grandpa had

loaded the equipment in the truck, Jodie had put Lady away in the barn and was waiting at the gate. Grandma looked at her doubtfully. "Jodie," she said softly, "this might not have a happy ending, you know. Maybe you should wait in the house."

Jodie shook her head. "I found the cow. She's expecting _me_ to come back and help her. Besides, you need me to show you exactly where she is."

"Get in, Jodie," Grandpa said, opening the door for her.

They drove slowly through the darkening woods with Jodie giving directions. Twice they had to stop while Grandpa sawed trees out of the way. At last the truck lights picked up the shape of the huge, bushy, fallen tree. "That's it!" Jodie yelled.

The three of them piled out of the truck and went to investigate. Grandma shone the flashlight in through the branches while Grandpa crawled as far under as he could. "Easy, bossy," he said comfortingly.

"Moooo!" the cow said.

Grandpa crawled back out. "Well?" Grandma asked in a worried voice.

"At least the trunk didn't hit her," Grandpa said. "She's not crushed. The big branches have kept most of the weight off of her, but she's got some bleeding spots and I can't tell if she's broken any legs. We'll have to saw our way in." He went to get the chain saw from the back of the truck.

Jodie crawled in among the branches. "See, cow, I told you I'd get help. You just hang tough now. Grandpa will get you out." The cow mooed softly. Jodie got out of the way and Grandpa started the saw. Its roaring filled the quiet night as sawdust flew and chunks of trunk and branches fell. Grandma and Jodie threw them back away from the tree. At last the cow was free from her prison. The huge branches that had surrounded her were all gone.

Grandma spoke softly and gently ran her hands over the cow's back and legs.

"What do you think, Ellen?" Grandpa asked.

Grandma shook her head doubtfully. "I don't feel any broken bones, but she's got a couple of wounds where sharp branches stabbed her, and maybe some cracked ribs.

But it's hard to say what internal injuries she could have."

Grandpa nodded sadly. "Yeah, she's definitely hurt. She'd have got up by now if she could. There's nothing holding her. I guess the kindest thing to do is . . ."

"No!" Jodie shouted. "Please don't kill her! She managed to survive under there for two days just waiting for someone to come and help her. Now she at least deserves a chance to live. Please give her a chance, Grandpa!"

Grandpa and Grandma looked at each other. Grandma sighed. "Well, she doesn't seem to be suffering much."

"No," Grandpa agreed, "she's not too uncomfortable here. Tell you what, Jodie. We'll try an experiment. After all that time under the tree this old cow should be real hungry and thirsty. We'll go back and get her a pail of water and some hay. If she eats and drinks, it'll mean there's hope for her. If she doesn't . . ."

Jodie nodded. "Okay, Grandpa. I'll stay here and keep her company."

Jodie sat alone in the dark forest and

watched the tail lights of the truck disappear down the trail. Then she moved close to the cow's big warm body. "Cow," she said softly, stroking a long, silky ear, "you eat and drink if it kills you, hear?"

"Moo," the cow replied.

Soon Grandma and Grandpa were back. Grandma was carrying a big pail of water. Grandpa had a bale of good green hay. He offered the hay to the cow. She sniffed it and turned her head away. Grandpa shook his head. Jodie felt the tears stinging behind her eyes. No, cow! You can't give up. Then an idea hit her. If *she* had been trapped under a tree for two days, what would she want first? "Grandma!" she yelled. "Give her the water first! Her mouth's too dry to eat hay."

Grandma set the bucket down in front of the cow's nose. The cow started to turn her head aside again. Then she sniffed. And sniffed again. Suddenly her long neck reached out and she stuck her nose into the bucket and began sucking up water like a high-powered vacuum cleaner. She inhaled every last drop and looked around for more. Grandma brought another bucket. It was instantly slurped up, too. Then Grandpa offered the hay again. The cow went to work on it like a kid with cotton candy.

Grandpa reached a strong arm around Jodie and the other around Grandma. "Good work, gang!" he said. "She'll be fine out here for the night. Let's go see what *we* can find for supper."

Jodie went around in a cloud of happiness all evening feeling like a knight who had saved a damsel in distress. But deep down she knew that Tree Cow, as she'd begun to call her friend, wasn't really "out of the woods" yet. Eating and drinking were one thing. Getting up and walking were another.

All week, morning and evening, Jodie helped take breakfast and supper out to Tree, who ate everything in sight, drank all her water, and chewed her cud contentedly. But she didn't get up.

"You know, Jodie," Grandpa said one day, "this can't go on forever. It's fine while the chinook holds, but if it gets real cold we can't let Tree just lie there and freeze to death."

Jodie nodded and tried to swallow the lump in her throat. Please, Tree, try.

The next morning was Saturday and Jodie slept in. She was awakened by Grandpa gently shaking her. "Hurry up and get up, Jodie-kid. You've got company waiting outside." Jodie rubbed her eyes, wondering if it was Eric come to ride with her. She jumped into her jeans and sweatshirt, but took time to tie her hair back with a pink ribbon just in case it was Eric.

When she hurried out onto the step, there was no one in sight except Grandpa. Jodie looked up and down the lane. She still couldn't see anyone. Grandpa chuckled. "You're looking in the wrong direction, Jodie-kid," he said and gently turned her head towards the barn. There, looking a little skinny and shaky but standing on her own four feet, was none other than Tree!

"She walked in all on her own," Grandpa said. "She was waiting for breakfast when I got up."

"Oh, Tree! You wonderful, crazy old cow!" Jodie yelled, rushing out to give her a hug.

"Moo," said Tree, and began to chew her cud.

OLD OBNOXIOUS
AND THE STRAY

It was March already, but the December dog tracks were still frozen in the snow. All winter they had stayed, reminding Jodie of the big, beautiful dog who no longer walked these trails. But now, even as Jodie watched, the warm spring sun was erasing the pictures from winter's slate. Slowly the icy outline of a pawprint softened, blurred, and began to weep away into a tiny river of meltwater that rushed away to join a million other little streams all rushing towards summer.

Go ahead, Jodie thought, wash them away. Wash all of Storm's tracks away. I don't want to see them any more. I want to forget her. But deep down Jodie knew that was a lie. How could she ever forget Storm? Storm, the big, black-and-tan German Shepherd who had lived on Jodie's grandparent's ranch since before she was born. Jodie had somehow expected that Storm would always be a part of the ranch just like the rolling foothills and the creek that rippled through the bottom of the pasture. But animals aren't like hills and creeks. They get old. They die. Storm had died in January. Since then the ranch had been a lonely place.

Jodie couldn't think of anything she wanted to do outside. Slowly, kicking at the slushy snow, she wandered back to the house to see what Grandma was up to.

Grandma was busy doing the ranch's bookkeeping for the month. She didn't have time to visit. She did look up when Jodie wandered in. "Nothing to do, Jodie?" she asked.

Jodie shook her head.

Grandma looked out the window. "Beautiful day out there. Why don't you take a walk?"

Jodie shrugged. "Nowhere to walk to."

This time Grandma laid down her pencil and gave Jodie a long, thoughtful look. "Or nobody to walk with? You're still missing Storm, aren't you?"

Jodie sniffed back the tears that still threatened to escape whenever she talked about the dog. "I guess so, Grandma."

Grandma got up and stretched and came over to put a strong arm around Jodie's shoulders. "Grandpa and I miss her, too, you know. You can't love an animal all her life without feeling bad when she's gone. It's okay to save a special place in your heart for Storm, but you've got to go on with the rest of your life, too. Now, why don't you get yourself a cookie and then go out and take the stray for a walk? I'm sure she's sick and tired of being tied up."

Jodie sighed. Taking the stray for a walk was worse than walking without any dog. All she did was remind Jodie of how much nicer a dog Storm had been. But Jodie helped herself to a still-warm sugar cookie and trudged back outside.

The black and white dog lay watching her

23

from outside Storm's old house where Grandpa had tied her up. Jodie had been really angry that Grandpa had even let this newcomer *use* the doghouse. It was *Storm's* house. This dog had wandered in about a week ago, muddy and footsore and half starved. She had no collar and no one around the ranch had ever seen her before. Grandma had put an ad in the paper to try to find her owner, but no one had phoned about her. Jodie didn't think anyone ever would. No one would *want* this dog back. Grandma and Grandpa would end up keeping her forever.

Jodie walked reluctantly toward the dog. When the dog realized someone was coming to talk to her, she leaped to her feet and stood whining with eagerness, straining at the end of her chain. Grandma was right about her being sick of being tied up. Obviously she hated it. But with the cows calving, an untrained dog running around loose was a real nuisance.

And this dog was *untrained*. She had no cow sense at all. It wasn't that she was *mean* to the cows. She *loved* cows. In fact, at times it seemed like she thought she *was* a cow. She was forever trotting through the herd trying to give the new calves doggy kisses on their noses. It gave their mothers nervous breakdowns!

Once, Grandpa had decided that since the stray was so interested in cows maybe she was a cattle dog. Maybe she had been trained to chase them out of places they weren't supposed to be. So when sneaky old Apron slipped into the hay corral while Grandpa was loading a bale, he called the new dog. She came galloping in full speed ahead, tail wagging, eager to help. Grandpa pointed at Apron. "Get that cow out of there!" he told the dog. "Rowff!" the dog said, and set off after the cow.

There was only one problem. Any good cattle dog knows enough to get behind the cow and nip her heels. That gets her moving in the right direction. But not this dog. She ran straight up in front of the cow and started barking in her face like an angry baseball player arguing with the umpire. The cow blew through her nostrils and took a run at the dog. The dog dodged and came back with a quick nip on Apron's nose.

"BAAWWP!" Apron roared, so upset she charged right out of the corral — but not through the open gate. She knocked a big section of fence flat on the ground and Grandpa had to spend the rest of the afternoon repairing it.

Except for when someone took her for a walk, the dog had been tied up ever since.

Now, at the thought of getting loose, the dog was so excited she was almost turning herself inside out with wagging and wiggling and bounding up and down. "Settle down, dog," Jodie muttered, trying to get close enough to unsnap the chain without getting knocked right off her feet. "Sit!" she commanded in a stern voice. The dog rolled over twice and held up a paw to shake. Jodie just shook her head. When the brains were being passed out, this dog must have thought they said "trains" and got off the track.

Jodie unsnapped the chain and fastened the leather leash to the dog's collar. "Okay," she said grumpily, "let's go, Miss Dog." Grandpa had been trying to get Jodie to give the stray a proper name, but she wouldn't do it. Naming her came too close to adopting her, and Jodie didn't *want* this dog. So, since she had to call the stray something and about all she knew about the critter was that it was a female dog, Miss Dog would have to do for now. And, Jodie hoped, "for now" might be as long as this dog would be around.

As the dog practically pulled Jodie down the lane at the end of the leash, Jodie studied her. She might be a pretty enough dog if she was fed properly and had her coat groomed. She was mostly black, on the surface, with a sort of silvery undercoat, a white cross on her chest, and four white paws. Three of the white socks were short. The left front one extended almost to her knee (if dogs have knees) and was peppered all over with tiny black Dalmatian spots. It was her flashiest feature. Grandma had been sure to mention it in the newspaper ad.

Nobody could guess what breed of dog this one might be. Grandpa decided she was a "Heinz 57," which Grandma explained meant she was such a mixture of breeds nobody could sort it all out. Grandma had her own ideas, though. She said the colour and markings were border collie, but the shape of her body and her long, feathery tail were Irish setter. Grandpa agreed that the dog definitely had the brains of an Irish setter. Jodie didn't quite understand what he meant by that, but it didn't sound like a compliment.

"Slow down, Miss Dog," Jodie grumbled, "you're pulling my arm out of its socket." At the sound of her voice, Miss Dog glanced back over her shoulder, wagged her tail even harder, and trotted on with even more enthusiasm — and speed.

"Jodie!" Grandma's voice came from the front step of the house. With great difficulty Jodie winched the dog to a stop and called back. "Yeah, Grandma?"

"If you go by the barnyard, stop by the little corral and see if Old Obnoxious has had her calf yet. But *don't* go in the corral with her."

"Okay, Grandma."

Jodie took the dog out the pasture gate and on out to the field, where the cows and their newborn calves were sunning themselves on a warm hillside. Jodie loved to watch the sparkling clean red-and-white babies sleeping in the sunshine or playing "King of the Mountain" on a big mound of hay their mothers hadn't eaten yet.

Miss Dog strained at the leash, wanting desperately to get loose and do some calf-kissing, but Jodie held her firmly back. The last thing Jodie wanted was to be the special guest human in the middle of a cow-dog riot.

"Come on, Miss Dog," Jodie ordered. "Let's go check Old Obnoxious like Grandma said."

Like most of the named cows on the ranch, Old Obnoxious had earned her name. She had the disposition of a grizzly bear with ingrown toenails. *Nobody* messed with Obnoxious if they could help it, *especially* when she was feeling protective of a brand-new calf. She was the last cow left to have her calf, and Grandpa had shut her in the corral just to make sure the calf was safely born before she went out with the other cows. Grandma had looked Obnoxious over carefully before breakfast and announced that she was sure the calf would arrive today.

Near the corral, Jodie paused and tried to peer between the heavy rails. She couldn't see the cow from here. Obnoxious must be lying down. Jodie needed to climb up where she could get a better view. But what about Miss Dog? If Jodie let go of her, the dog would be sure to get in trouble. "You stay here," Jodie commanded, looping the leash around a fence post. Miss Dog whined and pulled on the leash but then gave up and sat down. Her eyes followed Jodie's every move as Jodie shinnied up the side of the corral to get a look at Old Obnoxious.

Jodie settled herself on the top rail — and suddenly froze. Down below her in the corral, a miracle was taking place. Old Obnoxious was lying stretched out on her side, breathing hard and making little moaning sounds. The muscles on the cow's side rippled — once — twice — three times. Then, out behind her slid a wet and steaming red-brown package.

Almost instantly the package began to stir. Tiny, still-soft hooves explored the air.

A miniature muzzle lifted, feebly at first, snuffling and snorting, wetly gasping for its first real breath of air.

Suddenly there was a great scrambling as Old Obnoxious came out of her daze and lurched awkwardly to her feet. She was throwing belligerent glances in all directions and making the funny little mooing noises all cows make to their newborn calves. Her nose touched the soggy, slimy calf, and she jerked back as though offended, only to reach out again. This time Obnoxious sniffed the strange little creature — and fell instantly in love. Excitedly, she began to lick the calf with her big rough tongue, drying, warming, and massaging him, urging him to stand up and get his first drink of warm, life-giving milk.

The calf tossed his head, shook his wet and bedraggled ears, and snorfled some more. He gave an awkward lunge upward, but got his too-long legs all tangled up and landed in a heap. Old Obnoxious gave a loud, alarmed bawl and started washing him all over one more time. A minute later, the calf tried to stand up again. Instinctively, like all

31

cattle, he raised the back end first and stood propped up on trembling hind legs while he tried to get his front ones unfolded. Again he collapsed into a pile of awkwardness.

Jodie found herself counting the tries. Six times the baby bull calf tried and fell. But suddenly, on the seventh, he was standing. Trembling with all four legs propped wide apart, he looked like a damp, red-brown upholstered sawhorse with a head attached. Jodie couldn't hold back a giggle as she watched from her perch. But the sound made Old Obnoxious shake her head and snort and throw a red-tinged glare in Jodie's direction. Instantly, Jodie clammed up.

The calf took a wobbly step forward. Then another. His small pink nose reached out, searching. Eagerly, he bumped his nose up and down his mother's side before settling into vigorously sucking the cow's "armpit" just behind her front leg. No, you idiot, Jodie scolded silently. Not there, you brainless child! Move back. The milk's in front of the *hind* leg.

The calf must have been a mind reader. With a sort of disgusted toss of his head, he abandoned his unsatisfactory lunch counter and stumbled along his mother's side. Here and there along her belly he gave a hopeful little nudge. Each time his pink muzzle came away disappointed — until at last it bumped against the cow's milk-filled bag. Hmm, this smelled more promising. He gave it a more thorough inspection, nosing about until — hey, what was this? Something just the right size to fit into a calf's mouth. He latched onto the teat with hungry determination. Instinct took over. He began to suck on it. Warm, delicious milk began to seep into his mouth. He swallowed. With the milk, strength flowed into his body. His sucking movements became stronger. His tail began to twitch.

Old Obnoxious turned her head around and began to gently lick the base of his spine. Her eyes were half closed with contentment and she looked less obnoxious than Jodie could ever remember . . .

At that moment one of Jodie's rubber boots fell off. She leaned forward and made an automatic grab for it as it dropped into the corral. As she did, the muddy bottom of her other boot slid — and lost its grip on the fence rail. Jodie tried to throw her weight backward, but it was too late. It all felt like it was happening in slow motion, but it took just a split second for Jodie to plunge from the top rail and down into the corral.

One ankle twisted under her as she landed. "Ouch!" she groaned, but fear froze the sound in her throat. She was looking straight into the murderous eyes of Old Obnoxious. The cow snorted and pawed at the ground, crazy-mad at the thought that *something* had tried to pounce on her new calf. Jodie swallowed hard and mentally measured the distance between herself and the cow against the distance to the safety of the fence. The cow was closer. Way too close. Especially since Jodie wasn't sure her twisted ankle would hold her up. The cow bobbed her head up and down menacingly. Her muscles tensed, ready for a charge.

Jodie did the only thing she could. "Help! Help me!" she screamed at the top of her voice, but even as she did she knew it was hopeless. Even if Grandma could hear her from inside the house there was no way she could get here fast enough. Grandpa was away helping a neighbour this morning. I'm on my own, Jodie thought, her mind half numb with terror. She closed her eyes as the cow began to move.

But all of a sudden a tremendous commotion made her open them again. A fierce black tornado that was all teeth and fur came rocketing under the bottom rail and shot between Jodie and the cow. "Miss Dog!" Jodie gasped as the stray leapt straight at the charging cow and sank her teeth right into its big wet nose. "M-a-a-a-w!" the cow roared, turning aside and shaking her head wildly to dislodge the dog.

Jodie's brain came to life. Now was her chance. She gathered her feet under her. Ow, that ankle *did* hurt, but it held her up. She scrambled for the fence. A split second later she was safe on the top rail. She glanced down just in time to see the dog let go and make a hasty retreat out of the opposite side of the corral with the angry cow just a hair's-breadth behind. Miss Dog slid under the bottom rail and the cow banged into the fence so hard that even Jodie's side of the fence shook a little.

Old Obnoxious swept a fierce glare around the corral. There, that was better. She had cleaned all those intruders out of her baby's nursery. The red fury faded from her eyes. She ran a long tongue up over her nose and cleaned up the little trickle of blood the stray's bite had left behind. Then she gave a gentle, motherly moo, walked back to her bewildered baby, and calmly began to give him yet another bath.

Jodie sighed with relief. Shaking, she climbed down the outside of the corral. Not until she reached the ground did she remember she was missing a boot. But something told her this wasn't a good time to go back for it. She was afraid Grandma was going to have one very dirty sock to wash.

All of a sudden something almost knocked her over. It was the stray, leaping up to plant eager, dog-breath kisses all over her face and muddy paw prints all over her clothes. She really *was* the worst-mannered dog in the world!

But right then Jodie threw her arms

around the worst-mannered dog in the world and kissed her back. She didn't care *how* dirty she got. "Miss Dog," she whispered into the thick fur, "you saved my life." But then a thought struck her. She pushed the dog back far enough to get a good look at her. "But, you were tied up. How did you get loose?" Jodie ran her hand around the stray's collar and down the stub of leash still attached. It was soaking wet and imprinted with teeth marks all along the jagged break. The other end still hung from the post where Jodie had tied it.

"You chewed yourself loose to come and help me," Jodie said in a hushed voice as she wrapped the dog in yet another hug. "Oh, Miss Dog, you're the most wonderful dog in the world."

Miss Dog. It wasn't such a bad name. Not a bad name at all for a dog you loved and respected with all your heart.

THE STOLEN RIDE

The bale yard that had bulged with big silver-green bales of sweet-smelling hay was almost empty. Grandpa looked at it and shook his head.

"We'll have all we can do to stretch that hay to last another two or three weeks till the green grass grows," he said. Then he glanced at the five horses busily stuffing themselves with hay. "You know, Jodie, there's enough of last year's grass in the big pasture for the horses to dig out for a week or two. They use their hooves like shovels to scrape away the snow. Cows can't do that with their split hooves. I think we'll have to turn the horses out there and save a little more hay for the cows.

Jodie stared at him in disbelief. "Turn *all* the horses out? Even Lady?"

Grandpa grinned and ruffled Jodie's hair. "I know you practically eat and sleep with that horse, Jodie-kid, but don't you think you could get along without her for a little while? All the horses will come up to the salt lick every few days. You could catch her then and have a ride.

Jodie sighed and managed a grin of her own. "Okay Grandpa, if we really need the hay for the cows, I guess I can get along."

"Atta girl! Go grab your bridle and you can ride Lady out to the big pasture. The other horses will follow her."

"No saddle?" Jodie asked.

"Not unless you want to carry it home on *your* back after you turn Lady loose out there."

"No way!"

Grandpa boosted Jodie onto Lady's back. Lady was fat and covered with a thick mat of winter hair. She felt like a well-padded sofa. Jodie headed out toward the big pasture. Grandpa walked around behind the other horses, getting them started. Soon they had fallen into a long line, all obediently following where Lady led. Jodie glanced behind her and then turned to pat Lady's neck. "Way to go, Lady! You may be the smallest horse but you've sure got those other guys put in their place." Lady bobbed her head up and down as if she understood every word.

At the big pasture gate Jodie stopped and waited for Grandpa to catch up. He opened the gate and Jodie rode through with the rest of the horses still playing follow-the-leader behind.

"Okay, Jodie, slide off. End of the line for us," said Grandpa.

Jodie did. She unbuckled the throat strap on Lady's bridle. Then she lay her cheek against Lady's velvet nose. "I'm gonna miss you so much, Lady." Lady nuzzled her gently, obviously saying, in horse, that she was going to miss Jodie, too.

Meanwhile, the other horses had noticed they were in a nice big new territory. They were sick of hanging around waiting. One by one they slipped past Lady and began exploring the big pasture. Finally, Flame, Grandpa's blaze-faced sorrel, stuck her nose to the ground, gave an excited snort, and set off at a trot up the trail toward the field. She had remembered where the best grass grew. The other horses took off at a trot, too.

Suddenly Lady forgot all about how she was going to miss Jodie. She jerked her head high in the air and let out an ear-splitting whinny after her disappearing friends.

"Better turn her loose, Jodie, before she turns herself loose," Grandpa advised.

Reluctantly, Jodie pulled off the bridle. Lady gave a toss of her head, a loud snort, and was out there like she'd been shot from a cannon. The last glimpse Jodie caught before the black mare rounded a bend was of her bucking and kicking like a rodeo bronc.

Grandpa laughed and put an arm around Jodie's shoulders. "Everybody likes a little freedom now and then," he said.

For the next few days Jodie tried to find things to do that didn't involve riding Lady.

Of course school took up a big part of the day, but as the bus neared home Jodie always caught herself planning how she would get these school clothes off, put on her pleasantly dirty, patched jeans and race off to catch Lady — until she remembered.

On the fifth day of Ladygone, Grandma met Jodie at the door. "Grab a couple of my sugar cookies and then hurry and change your clothes," she said. "I was just down along the pasture fence half an hour ago and I saw all the horses at the salt block. Now's your chance for a ride."

"Thanks Grandma!" Jodie planted a kiss on Grandma's cheek, helped herself to four cookies, and two minutes later was headed for the barn.

Ten minutes later she had her bridle and an ice-cream pail full of oats and was standing at the salt block in the big pasture, very disappointed. The horses were gone. There were fresh tracks all over the place but not a horse in sight. Well, Jodie thought, if Grandma saw them half an hour ago, they can't be far. She threw the bridle over her shoulder, took a firm grip on her oat pail and, pretending she was a sharp-eyed Indian scout, set off to track the horses down.

The snow was almost melted now and the trail was clear on the muddy ground. The horses were heading toward the field, their favourite grazing spot. Jodie groaned to herself. It was a long way to the field. If she had to follow them all the way there, her walk would take more time than she'd have left to ride.

Just then she rounded a bend in the trail and came in sight of the spring that bubbled ice-cold water out of the ground. Sure enough, all that salt licking had made the horses thirsty. They were all gathered around drinking and nibbling the fresh green shoots of grass that were starting to grow near the water. Heads came up and ears leaned forward at the sound of Jodie's footsteps.

"Easy guys," Jodie soothed. "I'm not a wolf. I'm the oat lady. Come and get 'em!" She rattled her ice-cream pail. The horses stared a minute longer. Then they started to come toward her. Soon all four were gathered around pushing and shoving and demanding a share. "Wait your turn, Flame!"

Jodie laughed. "Get your nose out of the bucket, Copper. You had your share. Okay, Raintree, here's a bite for you. Come on, Lady, I'm saving you some."

Before Jodie knew it the four horses had devoured every bite of oats. Jodie held the bucket upside down. "All gone, guys," she announced. "No use tramping all over my feet, there just aren't any more. Okay, Lady. Now we're going for a ride."

She stepped up beside the little black mare and started to slip the bridle onto her head. Lady reached a questioning nose toward the oat bucket. It really *was* empty. She was *not* impressed. With a disgusted snort she took a step backward.

"Hey, Lady, be nice," Jodie scolded. She took a step toward Lady. Lady took two fast steps back. "Lady!" Jodie made a fast grab for Lady's mane. That was a mistake. Like a wild mustang, Lady whirled away on her hind feet and trotted to the edge of the little clearing.

There she stood, head up, nostrils quivering, just daring Jodie to make a move in her direction.

Jodie couldn't believe this. At home she could hardly keep Lady out of her back pocket, she was so tame. Lady was enjoying her freedom out here just a little *too* much. Jodie took a slow, easy step in the mare's direction. Lady turned and started walking away. Jodie sighed. It was no use. She wasn't going to catch her here. If only she was back at the barn, it would be so easy.

Raintree, the big buckskin, was nosing Jodie's shoulder. She wasn't the least bit worried about being caught. Jodie never rode *her*. Jodie had wanted to try, but Grandma had always insisted that Rainy was just too big a horse for Jodie to handle. Jodie had never really believed it. The one time Grandma had boosted her on the buckskin for a ride around the corral Rainy had obeyed perfectly. Absent-mindedly, Jodie stroked the buckskin's nose. Slowly, a plan began to take shape.

Coming out to the big pasture, all I had to do was ride ahead and the other horses all followed, Jodie remembered. So, if I got on a horse and rode toward home all the horses would follow again and I could get Lady into the small pasture and catch her. Why not? Grandpa had once told Jodie that in order to catch a horse you had to be smarter than the horse.

Jodie unfastened the buckles on the bridle and made it as big as she could. There, that looked about right for Rainy. "Whoa, Raintree," she said, in her most confident voice. Raintree stood peacefully, head down, and let her slip the bit between her teeth. Jodie gently pulled the bridle over Raintree's ears, straightened her mane, and buckled the throat latch. She might not have Lady but she sure had caught herself a horse.

Now, she thought, looking *way* up at Raintree's broad back, how do I get on? The answer was standing nearby. A big, flat-topped stump. She led Rainy up beside it. "Whoa, girl." Jodie clambered up onto the stump. Raintree waited patiently. Jodie stretched her right leg across Raintree's broad back, settled herself comfortably astride it, and took a clump of mane in one hand and the reins in the other. She was in business.

She gave the big mare's sides a gentle

squeeze with her knees and Raintree moved obediently forward. Jodie turned her toward home. "Come on, horses," she called as she rode off.

A little way down the trail she stopped and looked back. The horses weren't coming. She took Raintree back to them and started off again. No luck. Raintree just wasn't a leader like Lady had been.

Speaking of Lady, Jodie caught a glimpse of her over her shoulder. The little black mare had turned and was starting to walk down the trail in the *opposite* direction. Flame and Copper looked first in Raintree's direction, then in Lady's. They chose Lady and turned to follow her.

"Hey! You can't do that! Don't follow her! Here horses! Here horses!" Jodie called desperately. The horses didn't listen. Jodie thought fast. Now what would Alex, the kid in the Black Stallion books, do? Give up? No way! He'd go round up those horses and *chase* them home. She nudged Raintree into a trot.

The buckskin was rough! Just staying on her took all Jodie's attention.

They caught up to the other horses. Now, Jodie thought, I'll just get ahead of them and make them turn around. But the other horses started to trot, too. She urged Raintree to a faster trot and tried to squeeze past the others on the narrow trail. They trotted faster, too. Suddenly the rhythm of Raintree's stride changed. She had broken into a gallop. It was much smoother but it was *fast*. Jodie tried to slow her down. But now the other horses were galloping, too. They were all going faster and faster, their hooves making thunder on the ground. Jodie was getting scared. She pulled harder on the reins. Raintree pulled back again, tossing her head and fighting the bit. Jodie was in big trouble.

Stay calm, Jode, she told herself. Just hang on and stay calm. The trail suddenly headed up a steep hill. The horses slowed a bit. Jodie pulled on the reins with all her strength. She felt Raintree's neck flex a little. She was obeying the bit. Jodie kept pulling. Raintree slowed to a trot. Then to a fast walk. The other horses were galloping again. Jodie couldn't wait any longer. She jumped off the still-moving horse, stumbled, and almost turned her ankle, but somehow kept her balance. She was still holding the reins.

"Whoa!" she commanded in her sternest voice. Raintree stopped moving. She threw her head up and sent a shrill and desperate whinny after her disappearing friends. "Stop it, Raintree! I'm going to turn you loose. Just let me get the bridle off."

But Raintree wasn't listening. She was having a fit at the idea of being left alone by the other horses. She pumped her head up and down. She wouldn't stand still. Jodie couldn't reach the buckle on the throat latch. What would she do if Raintree jerked free and ran away with the bridle on?

Suddenly Jodie spotted another big stump. Quickly she led Raintree over to it. Raintree whinnied again and tried to pull the reins from Jodie's hand. Jodie hung on tight and climbed onto the stump. Now she was as high as Raintree's head. With one swift movement, she undid the throat latch. Just as Raintree tried to pull away again Jodie grabbed the top of the bridle and pulled it forward over the horse's ears. The bit slipped from Raintree's mouth. For a second, Raintree stood absolutely still. Then she gave her head an experimental toss. Nothing was holding her. She was free! She ducked her head, gave a triumphant snort and took off like a racing car at Indianapolis. Chunks of dirt flew all over. Most of them landed on Jodie. Jodie didn't care. She was free, too.

Jodie walked back home slowly. She had really got herself in one fine pickle today. Now she understood what Grandma meant when she said that Raintree was "just too much horse for Jodie." Come to think of it, Grandma was right about a lot of things.

When Jodie walked into the barnyard carrying her bridle, Grandma was just finished with feeding the bulls.

"You didn't find your horse?" Grandma asked. "Too bad. Oh well, there are worse things than a nice walk."

Jodie nodded. "You've got that right, Grandma," she said.

BUT COWS CAN'T FLY

It happened the day Grandpa had the trouble with his appendix.

Monday morning Jodie woke before daylight to find Grandma gently shaking her shoulder. "Wake up, Jodie! We've got a bit of an emergency here."

Instantly Jodie was awake and sitting straight up in bed. "What's wrong, Grandma?" she asked, wide-eyed and worried.

Grandma gave her a pat on the shoulder. "Now don't you go getting yourself all upset, honey. It's not all that serious, but

Grandpa's got a pain in his side and I think it might be his appendix."

Jodie knew all about appendixes. Her best friend, Heather, had come down with appendicitis right in the middle of the school Christmas concert last year.

"Will Grandpa need an operation?" Jodie asked. She was trying to picture him sound asleep on the operating table, but in her mind she kept seeing him lying there wearing his stetson hat and cowboy boots.

"Well, he might," Grandma said, sounding tired. In *her* mind all she could see was one very grumpy Grandpa if he got stuck in the hospital for a week. "But we can't worry about that yet. Right now I have to run him into town and have the doctor check him over. Can you do the chores and get yourself off to school all right?"

Jodie's feet were already on the floor and she was reaching for her jeans. She felt really bad about poor Grandpa but she felt great about being trusted to manage things by herself here. "You bet, Grandma!" she said.

Ten minutes later, Grandpa had been hustled out the door. He was looking kind of pale and *very* grumpy and was muttering things under his breath that caused Grandma to say, "Harold! Watch your language!"

Grandma had reminded Jodie three times about Miss Dog's breakfast, the barn cats' food, the bulls' bale of hay, and even the wild bird seed for the chickadees. Then Grandma had reminded her *four* times to lock the house when she left and *not* to lock the key inside the house. Jodie had said, "I will, Grandma," and, "I won't, Grandma," in all the right places, while thinking to herself that at the rate Grandma was moving Grandpa's appendix might have to be removed right there in the kitchen. But now Jodie stood waving as Grandma wheeled the Buick down the lane. Grandma waved back. Grandpa waved, too — and scowled. Poor Grandpa! He wasn't going to make a very patient patient.

Jodie checked her watch. Forty minutes till bus time. She had to get to work. She fed the dog and cats, remembered the birdseed, and managed to heave and tug a heavy bale of hay from the stack and spread it out for the bulls to eat. One good thing, it was already the first week in May and the rest of the cattle were out grazing on fresh green grass. At least *they* didn't have to be fed. So it looked like all the chores were finished.

But Jodie suddenly remembered something Grandma had forgotten. Raccoon. Raccoon wasn't a raccoon at all. She was a cow. Well, actually a heifer, which is what you call a young cow before she has her first calf. And Raccoon was going to have her first calf soon. That was why she was shut up in the small pasture by herself. Grandma and Grandpa wanted to keep an eye on her to make sure she didn't have any problems.

Jodie gathered up a forkful of hay and carried it to the small pasture. Raccoon was walking up and down the fence looking lonely. "Come on, Coon!" Jodie called. "Here's your breakfast. Don't look so sad. Soon you'll have your very own baby to keep you company."

Coon gave Jodie a bored look that said she didn't believe a word of it and helped herself to a wisp of hay. Jodie checked her watch. Almost bus time. She'd better hurry.

On the bus Jodie sat next to her friend,

Eric, who lived on the next ranch. She told him all about Grandpa and how he might need an operation. Now that the excitement of being allowed to look after things by herself had died down, Jodie was getting really worried about Grandpa. Her worry must have showed on her face because Eric reached over and gave her an awkward pat on the arm, accidentally knocking her books on the floor as he did. "Don't worry, Jode. He'll be okay. My grandpa had his whole gall bladder out and Grandma said he was just as ornery as ever afterward. If you need any help with the chores, let me know."

Jodie swallowed a giggle as she bent to pick up her books. Eric was such a klutz sometimes. But he really was nice — for a boy, that is.

The morning at school dragged by like it was wearing lead running shoes as Jodie waited, and wondered, and worried. Then, just as the noon bell rang, her name was called over the intercom. "Please come to the office," the secretary said. With her heart pounding so hard she could hardly breathe, Jodie walked out of the room. She caught

Eric's sympathetic look as she passed his desk and managed a weak smile in his direction.

As soon as the classroom door closed behind her, Jodie broke into a run. She skidded around a corner in the hall so fast she very nearly collided with Mr. Burnaby, the janitor, who was pushing a big pail of soapy water on a cart ahead of him. "Whoops!" she burst out, swerving like a race-car driver and just missing an unexpected bath. "Sorry, Mr. Burnaby!"

She arrived at the office out of breath and the secretary handed her a message. Grandma had phoned. Yes, Grandpa *did* need to have his appendix out, but it was nothing to worry about. Just a routine case, according to the doctor. Grandma would stay at the hospital until he woke up after the operation, which might be quite late. Jodie was supposed to go home and do the afternoon chores and then ride right over to Eric's place to wait for Grandma. Eric's mom was expecting her.

The rest of the day dragged by. At last Jodie was on the bus, going home. They were almost to Eric's place. "As soon as I change my clothes, I'll get my horse and ride over to see if you need any help with the chores," Eric said, gathering up his books.

"Okay. There won't be any problems, but it'll be fun to ride back to your place together. See you later."

Ten minutes later Jodie was walking up her own lane. As usual, Miss Dog came bounding out to meet her. Today she was even more excited than usual. Nobody had been home *all* day, she announced in dog talk. It had been *very* boring. And she sure hoped Jodie had something exciting planned.

Jodie laughed and scratched the dog's ears. "Sorry, Miss, no excitement today. Just plain old chores."

Jodie changed into her old jeans and went out to do a replay of the morning chores. The cats, the dog, the bulls, and, last of all, Raccoon. Uh-oh, Jodie thought. That was a mistake. She should have checked Raccoon first. What if she was having her calf and there was a problem? She grabbed some hay and rushed to the small pasture, desperately hoping not to find Raccoon stretched out looking sick.

Jodie didn't find Raccoon in trouble. She didn't find Raccoon at all. At first Jodie couldn't believe her eyes. The small pasture was no bigger than a city-block square and there were only half a dozen trees in it. You couldn't miss seeing a cow in there, could you? Obviously, you could, Jodie thought.

She set down the hay and walked slowly back and forth through the pasture. Raccoon was not behind the shed. She was not drinking at the creek. She was not lying in the shade of the trees. Jodie found herself checking behind an old rotten log about big enough to hide a rabbit. There was no rabbit. There was no Raccoon, either. Jodie walked all around the fence. There were no holes. She double-checked the gate. It was closed and chained. What was going on here?

Jodie was still standing staring across the empty pasture when Eric came loping up on Frostface, his white horse. He got off, opened the gate, and came over to Jodie. "Hey, lighten up," he said. "You look like you just lost your last friend."

Jodie swung around to face him. "It's worse! I've lost my cow."

Eric scratched his head. "Huh?" he said with a puzzled grin. "How could anybody lose something as big as a cow?"

Jodie gave him a dirty look. "It's not funny, Eric. Raccoon was in this pasture when I left for school. Now she's gone and the gate's shut and there aren't any holes in the fence. The only way she could have got out is over the top."

Eric eyed the rail fence that stood higher than their heads. He shook his head. "Couldn't have jumped it."

"Yeah? Then unless cows can fly we've got an invisible cow somewhere in this pasture."

Eric thought a minute. "Maybe somebody stole her."

Jodie shook her head. "I already thought of that. There aren't any tracks going out the gate."

"You're right," Eric muttered, "but there's got to be an answer. Somewhere here there's got to be an answer." He paced around the fenceline, still muttering. Then, all of a sudden, he stopped by the creek, stared hard at something, and then yelled, "That's it!"

"What's it?" Jodie asked.

"The answer! I've got the answer! Come here. I'll show you."

Jodie went over to where Eric was standing. She didn't see any answers. All she saw was the slow-moving creek rippling its way under the fence and off into the big pasture. "Look!" Eric was pointing at the bottom fence rail. "What do you see?"

"A fence rail?"

"Yeah, a fence rail, but what do you see *on* the rail?"

Jodie took a closer look. "It looks like hair," she said.

Eric nodded. "Right! *Cow* hair!"

"You think it's Raccoon's hair?"

"You bet it is. Now look at this." Eric pointed to the soft ground at the edge of the creek. A perfect cow track was imprinted there in the mud.

Jodie was doing her best to think like a detective. So there was a cow track at the edge of the creek and cow hair on the lowest rail where the fence passed over the creek.

What did it all add up to? Suddenly, the pieces all fit together. "I've got it, Eric! Raccoon waded into the middle of the creek, then upstream to where it went under the fence. Then she scooched down to squeeze under the fence and rubbed off some hair on her way."

Eric nodded. "Bet you a million bucks we find her tracks coming out of the creek on the other side of the fence."

Five minutes later Eric would have had his million bucks. A clear trail of cow tracks climbed out of the creek and headed purposefully off into the thick brush of the big pasture.

Jodie shook her head. "That sneaky Raccoon! After I gave her a nice breakfast and everything. Why'd she want to get out so bad?" And then, before Eric could answer, Jodie had her own answer. "Oh, great! Grandma says cows like a real private place to have their calves. Raccoon was supposed to have her calf anytime now."

"Should be lots of private places for her out there," Eric said, looking out at the acres and acres of brush that spread across the big pasture.

"Yeah, but this is Raccoon's first calf. That's why she was locked up. So Grandma and Grandpa could keep an eye on her in case she had any trouble. She might die out there alone in the big pasture. We've got to find her. Let's get our horses and see if we can follow her tracks."

"Can't follow tracks very well on a horse. We better walk."

Jodie shook her head. "We'll need the horses to chase her home when we find her."

Eric took another look at the thick groves of trees around them. "*If* we find her," he said softly. Jodie pretended not to hear.

Leading Lady and Frostface, Jodie and Eric walked slowly through the brush, their eyes on the ground. At first the trail was clear. The ground was soft and damp. Following Raccoon's hoofprints was as easy as reading the print in a book.

Then all of a sudden the single cow trail was joined by a dozen other cow trails. There were tracks all over the place, and there was no way of knowing which set belonged to Raccoon. Jodie stared at the ground in amazement for a minute. Then she looked up and realized where they were. "Oh, great," she groaned. "Coon's led us right past the place where Grandpa puts a block of salt out for the cattle. Every cow in the pasture has been here for a lick in the last day or two. We'll never sort out Coon's tracks again."

Eric thought for a minute. "Well, she's been heading south all the time. Maybe if we circle around to the south side of the salt lick we'll cut across her tracks alone again. It's worth a try."

Jodie gave him a tired smile. "*Anything's* worth a try," she sighed.

South of the salt they *did* come upon some tracks. *Three* sets of tracks, in fact. All the tracks were heading in different directions.

"*Now*, what?" Jodie asked.

Eric shrugged. "Beats me. Pick a trail and hope we get lucky."

"Okay," Jodie said, pointing to the one on the left. "Let's follow this and see where it goes."

The trail wandered aimlessly through the trees, out into a little meadow, over to a spring where the cow stopped for a drink, and then back into a rocky patch of forest — where the tracks disappeared completely on the hard ground. Jodie looked at Eric. He just shook his head. "I'm all out of ideas," he said. "Maybe Miss Dog will track her down."

Jodie glanced over to where the big black-and-white dog was making a determined effort to climb a tree in hot pursuit of a squirrel. Jodie sighed wearily. "Miss Dog couldn't track down a pork chop if it was tied around her neck," she said.

Eric laughed and they trudged on in the general direction the tracks had been taking them. Miss Dog trotted importantly in front, acting as if she knew exactly what she was doing. Suddenly there was a crashing in the brush just ahead.

"It's her!" Jodie yelled. "It's Rac . . ." The rest of the sentence trailed off as a big buck deer went bounding off with Miss Dog right behind him. "What'd I tell you?" Jodie muttered. The deer and the dog disappeared into the brush, and Jodie and Eric wandered on. Each waited for the other to admit their hunt was hopeless and they might as well go home.

Jodie caught a flash of black through the trees far ahead. Miss Dog was coming back, loping easily along, nose to the ground as she tracked them down. All of a sudden a loud *bawp!* shattered the forest silence. Miss Dog gave a startled yip and jumped sideways just in time to avoid being trampled by a red-and-white cow that came charging out of the shadows under the trees. The cow had a red mask on her white face that made her look very much like a cow-type raccoon.

"Coon!" Jodie yelled, breaking into a run and dragging her startled horse along behind her. By the time Jodie got close enough for a good look, Coon had given up chasing Miss Dog, who was sitting at a safe distance with her tongue hanging out in a big dog-grin. Coon was still parked in the middle of the trail, head lowered, snorting softly through her nostrils and looking about as fierce as a cow can look.

"Easy, Coon," Jodie said soothingly as she stopped to give the cow all the space she needed. This wasn't like Coon. She was usually a real pussycat.

A small sound in the shadows behind her caught Coon's attention. Coon looked back over her shoulder and mooed — a soft, gentle little moo this time. Jodie stared in the direction of Coon's gaze. There, almost hidden in the tall grass, lay a tiny, white-faced calf — with a red patch over just *one* eye. "Coon!" Jodie burst out, "you've had a baby pirate!"

Miss Dog gave an excited yip. Coon gave a warning *b-a-a-w!* Jodie and Eric climbed on their horses and slowly herded Raccoon and the Pirate toward home.

Jodie and Eric were a little late for supper at Eric's place, but they were there at the table by the time Grandma phoned. "Grandpa's fine," Grandma told Jodie. "He has to stay in the hospital for a few days, but I'll be there to pick you up in half an hour. Oh, and I don't suppose you remembered to check on Raccoon when you did the other chores?"

"Yes, Grandma," Jodie said very seriously, "I remembered Coon."

"Oh, good! I was a little worried about her. You know she's due to have her calf any day now."

"Yes, Grandma, I know."

"Well, thank goodness she didn't choose today. I'd better get going now. Anything else you need to tell me about right now?"

Jodie grinned. "Nothing that won't wait till you're home, Grandma."

THE PETUNIA BEAR

On September 26, the day after her birthday, Jodie began her career as a wildlife photographer. Ever since she got the fancy new camera for her birthday she had been photographing everything in sight. The cats got so nervous they hid under the couch whenever they saw her coming. Miss Dog thought being a star was great, but she got so excited that she ran up and kissed the camera when Jodie aimed it in her direction.

Finally Jodie gave up and cornered Grandma and Grandpa for her next victims. They complained that they weren't wildlife and quickly decided to walk over to visit the neighbours. Jodie sighed. "How am I going to become a great wildlife photographer when there's not a living thing in sight?"

Grandma thought a minute. "I'll help you out," she said. "I've got a bunch of beef fat in the freezer that I've been saving to feed the birds this winter. We'll put some out in the feeder now and I'll bet you have all sorts of birds to photograph in no time."

Grandma put the fat in the feeder just across the driveway from the house. Almost instantly a chickadee appeared. He checked out the fat, gave a loud *chick-a-dee-dee*, and sat down to eat. Within minutes three of his friends had heard the call to dinner and came winging in to join him.

"There you go, Jodie. All the wildlife you need," Grandma said with a grin. "Come on, Harold, let's go. You come too, Miss Dog. Jodie doesn't need you trying to chase the birds away." Miss Dog bounded excitedly up to Grandma. Going for walks was much more fun than birdwatching.

Grandpa came out the door. "Don't get in any trouble while we're gone," he warned.

Jodie just laughed. "How could I get in trouble birdwatching, Grandpa?"

Grandpa grinned and ruffled her hair with his big hand as he went by. "I don't know, Jodie-kid, but if there's a way I bet you can find it."

Jodie waved as Grandma and Grandpa and Miss Dog walked away down the lane. Then she settled herself in a comfortable spot and focused the camera on the bird feeder. The zoom lens was great. She could get close-up pictures without going close enough to scare the birds. She took a few shots of the chickadees eating. Then, there was a flash of blue as a blue jay came in for a landing. The chickadees scattered. "That wasn't very nice of you to chase the little guys out," Jodie scolded. The jay gave a loud squawk that sounded like he was scolding right back at her. "What a rude bird!" But, rude or not, he was a beauty. Jodie took a picture of him with a huge beakful of food.

Next, a downy woodpecker began hammering away at the fat with his beak just as if he was pecking a hole in a tree. Jodie got two really good pictures of him.

Before she realized it, an hour had slid by. Even wildlife photographers in the jungle deserved a break once in a while, she decided.

Inside the house Jodie sat down at the table to drink some juice and see what was on TV. A few minutes later she glanced out at the bird feeder to see if there were any new customers. She almost dropped her glass of juice. There, standing on his hind legs and helping himself to some fat, was the biggest, fattest, shiniest, blackest bear she had ever seen.

At first she couldn't believe her eyes. A bear in the backyard? It couldn't be. But then she remembered Grandpa telling about meeting a bear while walking through the woods a few years back, and the neighbours had seen one cross the road last summer. It was wild country around the ranch. There *were* bears. But Jodie had never counted on having one of her very own. She grabbed her camera and focused through the window on the bear. This wouldn't work. From here there was a lilac branch right in front of his nose. What would a *real* wildlife photographer do?

Jodie took a deep breath. She walked to the door and slowly, ever so slowly, turned the knob. She gave the door a gentle push. Jodie stepped cautiously out onto the porch. The bear kept right on eating. Jodie started to pull the door shut behind her and then changed her mind. Even courageous wildlife photographers needed an escape route. She made sure the door remained wide open.

She raised the camera, zoomed in on the bear, and almost scared herself to death. The whole viewfinder was filled with a close-up of black nose, pink tongue, and *huge* white teeth. "Oh, wow," Jodie whispered, "what big teeth you have, grandmother!" Then she remembered she was a fearless photographer and began taking pictures. They were great shots. The bear chewing, the bear with a gob of fat on the end of his nose, the bear pausing to scratch his chin. There was only one picture left on the film.

Suddenly, the bear stopped eating. His nose twitched and he swung his big head from side to side as if he was trying to catch a disturbing scent. Then, looking straight at Jodie, he froze. "*Whoof!*" he said.

For a second Jodie froze, too. "Whoops!" she said. Then, quick as a mouse diving for its mousehole, Jodie slipped in through the open door and pulled it shut behind her. She was surprised to notice her hands were not quite steady as she set the camera on the table. "Whoa! That was scarey!" she said out loud. Then, another thought hit her. "Oh, I hope he's not a house bear." She stole a cautious peek out the window, half expecting to find the bear right there peeking in at her. But she was just in time to see him drop to all four feet and go loping off into the woods.

Right then Jodie stopped being scared — and started being proud. She was *some* photographer. On the first day of her career she had photographed a wild black bear. Next week it might be a Siberian tiger. She couldn't wait to get the film finished so she could see how her pictures turned out. She disturbed the napping cats for one more pose. Then she took the film out of the camera and waited impatiently for her grandparents to come home.

It seemed to take forever. Jodie was grateful

that the bear had gone in the opposite direction from the one they had taken. If he hadn't, she would have been *really* worried by now. When Grandma and Grandpa finally came strolling in, Jodie rushed out to meet them.

"Hi Jodie," Grandma said. "Did you get some bird pictures?"

Jodie grinned. "Oh yes, lots of them."

"Anything good enough for *National Geographic*?" Grandpa teased.

Right then some mischief skittered through Jodie's mind. "Well," she said thoughtfully, "there was one kind of out-of-the-ordinary."

"Oh? What'd it look like?"

"Real big and black."

"Oh." Grandpa sounded disappointed. "That'd be a raven."

"No, Grandpa, it definitely wasn't a raven."

"Probably a crow then."

"No, not a crow, either."

Grandpa scratched his head. "Hmm. Don't know what else it could be."

"Well," Jodie said, "I did get some pictures

of it. Can we run into town and get the film developed?"

"It's getting kind of late . . ." Grandma began, but Grandpa saved the day.

"Might as well. The afternoon's shot anyway. We'll drop off the film and then go get some pizza. Pictures should be ready by the time we've eaten."

For the first time in her life Jodie was the first one full of pizza. She waited impatiently for Grandma and Grandpa to finish eating. At last they drove back to the photofinishing place. Jodie piled out of the car and raced inside.

"How'd they turn out, Mrs. Gibson?"

Mrs. Gibson smiled. "One or two are out of focus, but generally they're a nice bunch of photos. Especially that big, black bear at the zoo. You can be very proud of your work, Jodie."

"Thanks, Mrs. Gibson." Jodie paused for a quick glance through the pictures. Yes! This was going to be *some* surprise.

In the car she handed the envelope to Grandma as Grandpa started the engine and headed for home. "Nice one of the woodpecker," Grandma said. "Chickadee's a bit blurry." Grandma rambled on with her comments, going through the pictures so slowly that Jodie thought she was going to explode with the tension.

Then, "What?" Grandma exclaimed. "Good heavens! They've given you someone else's pictures. There's a *bear* in here!" She took a closer look at the picture. "But, that's *our* bird feeder! That's *our* lilac bush! That's *our* backyard. There was a bear in our backyard!"

"Yes, Grandma."

"What?" Grandpa exclaimed, craning his neck for a look at the picture.

"Harold! Watch where you're driving. You almost put us in the ditch!" Grandma scolded.

The rest of the way home, Grandpa watched where he was driving while Jodie did a lot of explaining. It took some talking to convince Grandma that she had not been taking foolish risks.

By the time they got home Grandma had calmed down but she went straight to work gathering up what was left of the fat and putting it back in the freezer. "The birds can try it again this winter after Mr. Bear is safely in bed," she said firmly. "Now I hope that's the last we see of our furry friend."

Jodie kind of wished she *would* see the bear again, but decided it was smarter to keep the thought to herself.

That night Grandma and Grandpa went to bed early and Jodie stayed up arranging her photos in her new album. When she had it all done she let Miss Dog in to sleep on her rug by the back door and went yawning off to her own bed. She read for half an hour and then she lay daydreaming about her future as a photographer.

The daydreams were just turning into night dreams when she heard a noise. It sounded like soft footsteps creeping down the hall. Jodie felt the hair on the back of her neck prickle. A burglar was in the house! Then her common sense told her that couldn't be. How could a burglar get past Miss Dog? True, Miss wasn't much of a watchdog, but at the very least she would have jumped up and kissed the burglar half to death and made a big commotion.

No, the footsteps didn't belong to a burglar. In fact, they sounded very much like the steps of Miss Dog herself. What was going on here? Jodie slipped out of bed and crept to her door. She opened it a crack just in time to see the end of Miss Dog's tail disappear into the bathroom. What? Miss Dog never left her rug at night. Jodie followed Miss into the bathroom. The dog was crouched down in a corner looking very much like she was trying to make herself disappear.

"Miss Dog!" Jodie whispered. "Have you lost your mind? Come on back to your rug this instant." Miss Dog whined and looked embarrassed, but she refused to move. "What *is* going on here?" Jodie muttered to herself as she tiptoed out to check the dog's sleeping place. She was just in time to catch a movement through the window. In the moonlight, a very big, very fat, very black bear was just sauntering down the back steps. He must have been right up on the porch, peeking in the window. No wonder Miss Dog was nervous!

Jodie watched, fascinated, as the bear

walked down the sidewalk, past the big living-room window, and then made his way up onto the deck outside the front door. He lumbered over to one of the flowerpots that Grandma had hung from the deck railing last summer and took a long, deep sniff of the frozen petunia that was still in the pot. Then he made his way to the next pot and did the same thing. He had worked his way through half the flowerpots when Jodie felt a touch on her shoulder and almost jumped out of her skin. She spun around to find Grandma behind her watching the bear, too. Grandma put a finger to her lips. "Thought something odd was going on when I found the dog in the bathroom," she whispered.

A minute later Grandpa tiptoed into the room and saw the bear on the deck. He shook his head in amazement. "Never had a bear that bold before," he said in a low voice. "You think I ought to shoot him, Ellen?"

Grandma gave him a startled look. "Shoot him? Of course not, Harold. You can't go shooting things in the dark. You might only wound him. Besides," she muttered, "how can you shoot something that just came to smell the flowers? We'll call the wildlife office tomorrow and see what they can do about him."

Right about then the bear finished checking out the last of the petunia pots, ambled down the steps, and waddled peacefully off into the forest. The three spectators ambled off to the kitchen to make hot chocolate since nobody was very sleepy anymore. On the way they met Miss Dog who was just coming out of the bathroom and trying not to look embarrassed about her performance as a big brave watchdog.

In the morning Grandma spoke to the wildlife officers. Just after noon their truck rolled into the yard, towing something that looked like a big steel road culvert. "Live trap," Officer Trenton explained. He put a nice chunk of spoiled bacon in the far end and attached it to a trip wire. "When friend bear comes in and grabs the bacon he releases the gate behind him, it falls into place, and presto, we've got ourselves a bear."

Jodie watched with interest as the officers

baited the trap. "Whew!" she said as they warmed the bacon a little with a torch. "He'll be able to smell that even if he's gone to B.C."

Officer Trenton laughed. "You could be right, Jodie. Bears have excellent noses. I'll bet he's out there in the woods not too far away just waiting till he thinks it's safe to come and have a snack. I don't think he'll show up till dark, though, after all the noise and commotion we made setting this thing up. But you all better stay in the house just to be on the safe side. Give us a call in the morning and let us know if our trap caught anything."

Jodie waited restlessly for darkness to fall. Then she and Grandma and Grandpa sat up and played Monopoly till almost midnight. Still they could see the door on the trap wide open in the moonlight. Grandpa yawned and stretched. "I think that bear's too smart to fall for that trick. Anyway, tomorrow's another day and I have to be up early." He went off to bed.

Grandma lasted another half hour. Soon she was almost asleep in her chair. "Well, I've run out of steam. The bear doesn't need me watching for him. Goodnight, Jodie. You'd better get some sleep, too."

"Night, Grandma." Reluctantly, Jodie gave up and went to bed, too. Her sleep was filled with bear dreams. She thought she was still dreaming when she heard a sound near her bed. Suddenly, she was sitting up, wide awake. The sound was real. It sounded like — heavy breathing! Jodie made a grab for the switch on the lamp. Light flooded the room. There, at the foot of the bed, lay Miss Dog, panting.

"Miss Dog! You've scared ten years off my life. What do you think you're doing off your rug again?" But before Miss Dog could answer, Jodie had her own answer. She heard another sound. This one was out in the yard and it was very loud. It was the clanging and banging of a very upset bear inside a trap. Jodie leaped out of bed. "Grandma! Grandpa! We've got company!"

Two minutes later they were all out peering, from a safe distance, through the steel mesh of the closed trap door. Two reddish eyes glowed back at them. The bear was well and truly caught.

"Well," Grandpa said, "he'll keep just fine till morning. The wildlife boys can come and look after him then. Everybody back to bed."

Jodie went back to bed but she didn't sleep much. She kept thinking about how happy her bear had looked when he was free to stroll around and smell the petunias.

The wildlife truck drove in shortly after ten the next morning. Officer Trenton took a look inside the trap and gave a low whistle. "That is some fine-looking bear you caught there, Jodie," he teased.

Jodie tried to smile but the smile came out kind of weak.

Officer Trenton smiled at her. "You're going to miss this bear, aren't you, Jodie?"

Jodie nodded. Then she asked the question that had kept her awake most of the night. "What's going to happen to him now? Do you have to shoot him?"

Officer Trenton shook his head. "Oh no, Jodie. Not this fellow. He's not a real troublemaker. He's just an adventurous young guy who chose a territory too close to civilization to explore. Your bear is going for a nice long trip out to the mountains. We'll turn him loose where there aren't any houses to visit. He should get along just fine out there."

Jodie was so relieved she felt like hugging Officer Trenton — or the bear. Instead she just stood grinning from ear to ear as the truck pulled away hauling the bear in the cage behind it. The bear had his black nose up against the back door taking one last look at the yard.

Jodie waved to him. "Happy trails, bear. Don't forget to smell the flowers!"

MR. WHO?

It was getting late. The early October twilight was already washing the blue from the sky. Jodie reined Lady to a stop and waited for her friend, Eric, to ride up alongside them.

"Guess we'd better be getting home before dark, huh, Jodie?" Eric asked.

Jodie nodded. "Yeah, I guess so," she said with a sigh. "I wish the days weren't so short at this time of year. I really did want to see what was over that next hill."

Eric studied the slope that stretched out ahead of them. "Just more trees, I bet. Same as on this side of the hill."

"Well, maybe," Jodie said. "But then again there could be an exciting discovery up ahead. You never know."

Eric laughed and started to turn his horse toward home. "Anybody ever tell you you've got an overactive imagination, Jodie?"

Jodie laughed, too. "Only about forty times a day." She nudged Lady with her knees and started to turn the mare around. Then, suddenly, she reined her in again. "Hey! What was that?"

Eric had already started down the trail. He stopped his horse and looked back over his shoulder. "What was what?"

"I don't know. I thought I saw something move up there along the fence near the top of the hill."

They both stared up the fenceline. "I don't see anything," Eric said. "Maybe a bird flew into the trees."

"Yeah, maybe," Jodie grinned. Or maybe it was my overactive imagination." She turned Lady onto the trail for home again. Then she took one last glance back up the hill. "I *did* see something!" she yelled as she spun Lady around and sent her loping up the hill. Eric's horse wheeled around and followed so fast that Eric was almost left sitting on thin air.

Halfway up the hill Jodie stopped and Eric caught up. Jodie looked puzzled. "I'm sure I saw it. Right near the fence up there." She and Eric both stared at the spot where she was pointing but in the dimming daylight all they could see were shadows.

"Maybe it was just the tall grass waving in the wind," Eric suggested.

"Maybe," Jodie said, "but I don't think so. Well, whatever it was it's gone now." She sighed, turning to Eric.

"No, it's not!" Eric said suddenly. This time he was the one to catch the movement in the shadows. "Let's go." They nudged their horses into a walk and moved slowly toward the mysterious spot.

As they came closer the pattern of light and shadow began to turn into a shape, the shape of a bird. A big bird with two huge yellow fog lamps for eyes.

"It's an owl!" Jodie said excitedly. "But why is he just standing there with his wings spread like that?"

"Shh," Eric whispered. "Don't scare him."

But with two people and two horses coming right at him, the owl was already scared. He flapped his wings hard. But he didn't go anywhere.

"Something's wrong with him," Jodie whispered, sliding off her horse for a closer look. The owl glared yellow fire at her, clacked his beak menacingly, and flapped his wings again, but still he didn't take off.

"Careful, Jodie," Eric warned. "Those things have fierce claws on them."

Jodie took a step closer. "What's wrong, owl? Are you hurt?" she said softly. The owl struggled again but not as violently as before. This time Jodie was close enough to see what was wrong. "Oh, no," she whispered. "Eric, he's got one wing caught in the barbed-wire fence. It's all torn up and bleeding."

Eric was beside her now. He shook his head. "Poor guy. He's really wrecked. Too bad we haven't got a gun."

Jodie spun around to stare at Eric. "A gun? What are you talking about, Eric?"

"You know what I mean. The only thing to do for a wild animal or bird that's hurt this bad is to put it out of its misery."

Jodie's eyes flashed. "Oh no it's not!" She peeled off her denim jacket. "Do you still have those wire cutters that you used to fix the hole in the fence?"

"Yeah, but . . ."

"Get them, quick. I'm going to wrap my jacket around him so he can't struggle and then you can cut the wire that's holding him."

Eric eyed the owl who was still clacking his beak fiercely. He looked awfully big with his feathers all fluffed out. "I don't know, Jode . . ."

"Eric, do I have to do this by myself?"

Eric sighed. "Okay, okay, we'll do it. But, here, at least put on my gloves. They're leather and he won't be able to get through them with his beak or claws."

Jodie put on the gloves and Eric got the wire cutters from his saddlebag.

"Okay," he said, "ready whenever you are."

Jodie nodded and took a step forward,

holding the jacket out in front of her. "Easy, owl," she said softly, meeting his hypnotizing yellow stare with a steady look from her own blue eyes. "Believe it or not, we're here to help you. Easy owl." Another step. The owl stayed still. The staring match continued. "Easy owl." Almost within reach. The owl started clacking his beak again. "Steady, owl. I hope your clack is worse than your bite." One more step — then Jodie pounced. The next thing the owl knew he was wrapped in the jacket. "Got him!" Jodie yelled. "Cut the wire quick, Eric!"

Eric reached in close to the struggling bundle. With a sharp *snap* the cutters sheared off the barbed wire. Eric did the same thing on the other side of the trapped owl's wing. And suddenly Jodie was holding an owl that was free — except for her firm hold on him. Gently, she lowered the jacket-wrapped bird to the ground and very carefully pulled back the jacket so the owl could look out. The yellow eyes blazed with renewed fury.

"Look at him, Eric," Jodie said softly. "He's hurt, trapped, probably half-starved, and scared to death, but he's still looking at us like he's the king of the castle and we're the dirty rascals! That is one proud bird. He needs a really dignified name." Jodie paused to think for a minute. "I think I'll call him Mr. Poindexter."

Eric's eyes were almost as wide as the owl's. "Mr. *Who*?" he squeaked.

Jodie burst out laughing. "Hey! That's better yet! Now all we have to do is get Mr. Who home where we can take care of him." Cradling Mr. Who gently in her arms, Jodie started for home.

"Hey, you aren't gonna *walk* all the way home, are you?

"I don't think I've got a choice. I can't ride a horse and hold an owl at the same time."

Eric thought a moment. "Sure you can. If I lead the horse. Here, let me have Mr. Who for a minute." He reached out and carefully took the jacket-wrapped bundle from Jodie. "Okay, get on Lady." Jodie climbed on. Eric handed the owl up to Jodie and, holding Lady's reins, climbed onto his own horse. Slowly, the strange procession made its way down the long trail back to Jodie's place.

It was pitch-dark when they rode into the yard. In the glow of the porch light they could see Grandma pacing back and forth outside the back door. At the sound of the horses she turned and came striding out to meet them. "Jodie Anne McCrimmon!" she said, her voice taking on the angry tone it always had when she was worried. "Do you know what time it is? You were supposed to be home an hour ago and . . ." Her voice trailed off as she spotted the bundle in Jodie's arms. "What on earth have you got there?"

"That's Mr. Who, Grandma," Jodie said, holding out the jacket-wrapped owl to her grandmother. "We saved his life. That's why we're late."

"Mr. *Who?*" Grandma said, reaching out to take the bundle.

"That's right, Grandma, Mr. Who. He's an owl and we found him with his wing caught in a barbed-wire fence." Jodie slid off her horse and carefully pulled back a corner of the jacket bundle her grandmother was holding. Two fierce yellow moons glowed in the night.

Grandma shook her head. "Well, for goodness' sake, it *is* an owl. A great grey owl. And here I always thought of them as such big birds. This fellow's light as a feather." She laughed softly. "Maybe that's because he *is* mostly feathers."

Just then the door opened and Grandpa stuck his head out. "Isn't *anybody* coming in so we can eat supper?" he asked. "My stomach's wearing a hole in my backbone." Then he caught sight of the bundle in Grandma's arms. "What have you got there, Ellen?"

Grandma sighed. "You'll find out soon enough, Harold. I think it just moved in with us."

An hour later the horses were fed and put away for the night, Grandpa's stomach — along with everyone else's — had been filled, and Mr. Who had his own apartment, a cage Jodie had used to take her bantam chickens to the fair last fall.

The microwave beeped and Grandma opened the door and brought out a dish of freshly thawed hamburger. "Here you go, Jodie," she said, "prime Alberta beef, but I don't think Mr. Who is going to like it."

"Oh, yes he is," Jodie said, scooping up a spoonful and reaching it in through the wire on the cage.

"He must be really hungry," Eric said.

"Here you go, Mr. Who, supper!" Jodie said.

The owl shrank back as far as the cage would let him, trying to get away from the spoon.

Jodie sighed. "Come on, Mr. Who. You're a 'highly skilled predator of the deep forest.' It says so right here in the bird book. Highly skilled predators don't try to escape from a spoonful of dead meat."

Grandpa looked up from his newspaper. "That's just the trouble, Jodie."

"What do you mean, Grandpa?"

"That owl *is* a predator. He's hunted his own meat all his life. To him, a mouse scurrying through the grass spells dinner. Showing him a spoonful of hamburger would be like handing a caveman a can of salmon and expecting him to understand it was food. It's just too far beyond his experience."

Jodie thought that over. Grandpa was

probably right. "Okay," she said, reaching for her jacket, "let's go, Eric."

Grandma shot them a sharp look. "Where do you two think you're going?"

"Hunting," Jodie said wearily.

"Oh, no you aren't!" Grandma's voice had taken on the no-nonsense tone that Jodie had learned not to argue with. "I've had a lot of critters in this house but live mice galloping around for the owl to chase is where I draw the line. Anyway, from the looks of the wound on that wing he needs a miracle more than he needs a mouse. I'm afraid we'll just have to . . ."

Suddenly Grandma got a thoughtful look on her face. She grabbed a pile of papers from the back of the table. "Now what did I do with that leaflet I picked up at the mall in Red Deer last month?" She leafed through the papers, muttering to herself. "Hmmph, I'm going to win a million dollars from this one. Yeah, me and everybody else in the country." She tossed that envelope in the direction of the garbage can. It missed. Grandma picked up another envelope. "Learn the simple trick of keeping aphids off your tomatoes in August," she read aloud. "Tomatoes?" she said with a snort. "Won't be aphids on them in August in this country. They'll freeze to death first." That envelope sailed into the garbage can. A perfect two-point shot. Grandpa caught Jodie's eye and winked. Grandma was a sight to behold when she finally got around to sorting papers.

"Here it is!" Grandma pounced on the leaflet she'd been looking for. "Medicine River Wildlife Rehabilitation Centre. Sounds like just what the doctor ordered for your Mr. Whoever. It's less than an hour's drive from here, too."

"Do you really think they could help Mr. Who?" Jodie asked.

"Well, I think they sure might give it a try. Says here they've rescued a lot of injured owls. There's a phone number here, too."

"Will you phone them, Grandma, please?"

Grandma shook her head. "No, I won't," she said. But before Jodie could say a word she added, "but you can. When you rescued the owl from the fence you took him on as your responsibility. Now it's up to you to carry it through."

Jodie stared at her and then looked over at Eric for support. Grownups were supposed to do the hard stuff — like talking to total strangers on the phone. But Grandma had picked up the phone and handed it to Jodie. "Here's the number. Go ahead and dial. Ask for a lady named Carol Kelly."

Jodie took a deep breath, organized her thoughts, and dialled the number.

"Medicine River Wildlife Rehabilitation Centre," a pleasant voice said. "May I help you?"

Jodie cleared her throat. "Uh, yes. Can I speak to Carol Kelly, please?"

"Just a minute, please. I'll call her."

Silence on the line. Then, "Hello, this is Carol Kelly."

"Hello, this is Jodie McCrimmon. We found an owl with his wing caught in a barbed-wire fence and we don't know what to do."

There was a short pause. "Where's the owl now, Jodie? Is it still in the fence?"

"Oh, no. He's not in the fence. He's in the kitchen."

"Oh." The lady sounded a little surprised. "How did you manage to get him free of the wire?"

"My friend Eric had some fencing pliers with him. We cut the wire."

"Good, Jodie. That was the right thing to do. Now, do you know where the rehabilitation centre is located?"

"Grandma knows where you are, I think." Grandma nodded.

"Okay. Can someone there drive up here with the owl right away?"

"Grandpa can, I think." Jodie gave Grandpa a pleading look.

Grandpa sighed like a tired man who had just eaten his supper late and would like to spend the evening with his feet up. But then he grinned at Jodie. "Get your coat on, kid. We're about to take a moonlight drive with an owl." Grandma grabbed her coat, too. "You comin' along, Ellen?" asked Grandpa.

"Well, of course, Harold," she said with a pretend scowl. "You know you'd be lost in ten minutes if I wasn't there to navigate."

"Can I come?" Eric asked.

Grandpa shrugged. "Why not? The more

the merrier. Phone your folks and ask them first."

Fifteen minutes later they were on the road, Grandma and Grandpa in the front seat of the Buick, and Jodie and Eric — with Mr. Who's blanket-covered cage between them — in the back.

The trip didn't seem very long. Finding the rehabilitation centre was easy — because of Grandma's expert navigating, of course. As they got out of the car a woman came to meet them.

"Hello," she said, "I'm Carol Kelly. You must be the people with the owl."

"That's right," Jodie said, carefully handing over the cage. "Here he is. His name is Mr. Who."

Carol smiled as she gently took the owl. "Well, hello, Mr. Who," she said very softly. "We're going to see if we can fix you up." She turned to Grandma and Grandpa. "If you have time you're welcome to come in and watch while I examine the owl and start on its treatment."

"Please, Grandma. Let's stay."

Grandma and Grandpa looked at each

other. Grandpa nodded and grinned. "Come on, Ellen. Let's see what we can learn about repairing owls. You never know when it might come in handy."

All four of them followed Carol and Mr. Who to the examining room. They watched as she put on heavy gloves and skilfully brought the owl out of the cage, weighed him, and fitted a plastic band around his leg. By now poor Mr. Who was so tired he had even given up clacking his beak. He just stared sadly at the world through his enormous yellow fog lamps.

"Can you make him better, Carol?" Jodie asked in a small voice.

Carol turned to look at Jodie. "I don't know, Jodie," she said gently. "He's had a serious injury and no one knows how long he was caught in the fence. He's pretty badly stressed but we'll do the best we can."

The others watched as Carol gave the owl an injection and then ran a tube into his beak and down his throat. "What's that for?" Eric asked.

Carol set a plastic pouch of liquid up so it drained down into the tube. "This is how we get some fluid into the owl right away. A bird that's been trapped and injured like this comes in terribly dehydrated and we can't wait till he feels up to eating on his own."

"We tried to give him some hamburger," Eric said, "but he acted downright scared of it."

Carol nodded. "That's a mistake a lot of people make. Trying to get an injured and terrified wild animal to eat. If one of us had been in a car accident and trapped in the car for days the last thing we'd want or need would be solid food."

"I guess we made a lot of mistakes," Jodie said.

Carol put a hand on her shoulder. "Don't feel badly about that, Jodie. You cared enough to do the best you knew how to help this owl. Just learn from your mistakes and next time you'll do even better. Okay, Mr. Who's got his medication and his fluids. Now what he needs is a warm, quiet place to rest. Come on, I'll show you the intensive care cage."

Carol took the owl to a cage and settled

him onto a big woolly blanket. "That looks nice and warm," Grandma said.

Carol smiled. "It ought to be. There's a heating pad under the blanket." She tucked the blanket around Mr. Who and dimmed the lights until it looked like two big yellow eyes were floating loose in the dimness. "What Mr. Who needs now is to be left alone. Being around people is really stressful for wild animals, so we'll bother him as little as we can until he starts to feel better."

"Goodnight, Mr. Who," Jodie said softly. "Please get better."

Mr. Who never said a thing but the yellow eyes glowed at her like beacons in the night. She took them as a promise that the owl would come back home some day.

On the car ride home Jodie drifted off to sleep. She dreamed of being out in the shadowy early-evening forest. She heard a swish of wings and looked up. A magnificent great grey owl was swooping past. "Who are you?" called Jodie.

"*Who!*" replied the owl. Jodie woke up feeling happy. Mr. Who *would* be back someday.

Every day for the next three weeks Jodie thought of Mr. Who and wondered how he was doing. Grandma said she could phone the rehabilitation centre, but Jodie wouldn't do it. She was sure it would be bad luck to ask. Carol had promised to let them know how Mr. Who made out. Jodie convinced herself that as long as they heard nothing from Carol, Mr. Who was still alive.

It was mid-November. Grandpa was reading the paper and Grandma was writing a letter when the phone rang. "You want to answer that, please, Jodie?" Grandma asked.

Jodie turned down the TV and grabbed the phone. "Hello?"

"Yes, could I please speak to Jodie McCrimmon?"

"That's me!" Jodie blurted out. Then, remembering the lesson on telephone manners they had in health class last year, she added, "Uh, speaking, I mean."

"Jodie, this is Carol Kelly from Medicine River Wildlife Rehabilitation Centre."

There was a long silence while Jodie took a deep breath and swallowed hard.

"Jodie? Are you there?"

"Yes, Carol," Jodie managed to say in a small voice.

"I promised to call you when there was any news about your owl."

"Yes?" Jodie's voice was almost a whisper this time.

"Well, you can get ready to celebrate, Jodie. Mr. Who has made a wonderful recovery. We moved him to the big flight cage today so he can exercise his damaged muscles and rebuild his strength to be released soon."

"No kidding!" Jodie's voice was almost a shout now. "He's really almost better?"

"He sure is. Feeling fine and eating us out of house and mouse. That's what we try to feed them, by the way. Mice, to keep their diet as natural as possible."

Hmm, Jodie thought, remembering how she was getting ready to go mouse hunting before Grandma put her foot down the night they found the owl. At least Jodie had been right about that.

Carol was talking again. "So, if all goes well, your owl will probably be ready for release in a couple of weeks. We'd like to put him back in his natural habitat close to where you found him. Could you show us the place?"

"You bet I could!" Jodie said with a huge grin.

On the last Saturday in November, a warm chinook breeze was eating holes in the thin early-season blanket of snow. The woods smelled of pine needles and echoed to the calls of jays and chickadees. Grandpa's old 4×4 farm truck was rumbling its way up the hill and into the deep forest. In the front with Grandpa were Grandma and Carol Kelly. In the back were Jodie and Eric and, safe in a cage, Mr. Who. The six of them were on an important mission.

Suddenly Jodie tapped on the back window. "Right here, Grandpa!" she called. The truck eased to a stop. Everyone got out. Eric carefully set the cage on the tailgate.

"Okay," Carol said, "who wants to release Mr. Who?"

Everyone turned to look at Jodie. "Mr. Who is Jodie's owl," Eric said. "She should do it."

Jodie shook her head. "Mr. Who isn't *anybody's* owl. He's a wild animal and he belongs to himself. But," she added with a grin, "I'll fight anybody for the chance to let him go."

Carol reached her gloved hand inside the cage and brought out the indignant owl. He looked fierce and insulted and much stronger than the last time Jodie had held him. Jodie reached for him, but Carol stopped her. "Not with your bare hand, Jodie. I don't want you for my next patient."

Eric gallantly held out his gloves to Jodie. "She never has her gloves when she needs them," he told Carol with a teasing grin in Jodie's direction. Jodie gave him an "accidental" jab in the ribs with her elbow as she reached out to take a firm but gentle hold on the owl.

"Okay, Mr. Who, just settle down. Look around, you silly bird. You're home. We brought you right back where you belong. And now we're going to let you go. Just promise me one thing," she said with a little catch in her voice. "Just let me know you're around once in a while, will you?"

"Ready now?" Carol asked. Jodie nodded. "Okay," Carol said, "just hold him up and let go. He'll figure out the rest."

Slowly, Jodie raised the owl into the air. Then she released her grip. For a second the owl balanced on her hand. Then he flapped his wings. And suddenly he was flying. With the speed and silence of a grey ghost he swept off into the shadows of the deep forest. Left behind were an empty cage and five people who could hardly believe he had ever been there.

But Jodie believed. Because, for the rest of the winter when she stepped out on cold, crisp, moonlit nights she often heard Mr. Who letting her know he was around. He always identified himself by name.

"*Who, Who, Who*," he said.

THE COMING OF
THE KATIE CAT

Winter's early snow lay in a thin, silver-white blanket across the woods and fields as Jodie and Grandma walked out to check the cows that day.

"It's almost too pretty to walk on," Jodie said, looking at the untouched sheet of white ahead of them.

Grandma nodded. "Yes, it is beautiful. But it's all right for us to put our footprints on it. Snow is Nature's writing paper, and every creature that goes out in the fresh snow leaves its signature behind."

Jodie gave her a puzzled look. "Signature?"

"Just keep your eyes open," Grandma said with a smile. "You'll soon see who has been out exploring this morning."

Jodie kept her eyes on the ground as they walked on. Suddenly she spotted a line of tracks crossing her path and heading toward the beaver dam. The tracks looked familiar. "Look Grandma. Miss Dog's autograph."

Grandma studied the tracks. "Well, they do *look* like dog tracks, but I think they belong to somebody else. Miss Dog hasn't been up here ahead of us yet. I'll bet her Cousin Coyote has been out on an early-morning mouse hunt. See how narrow these tracks are? Dogs have wider feet than coyotes." She pointed to another set of tiny tracks like embroidery stitches in the snow. "Chickadee's been out looking for breakfast."

Then Jodie spotted something that didn't look like a trail at all. More like a twisting tunnel that travelled just beneath the surface of the snow. "Okay, Grandma, bet you don't know who made *this* one."

Grandma chuckled and bent down for a closer look. "No problem, Jodie. This is Mr. Mouse's secret highway. Mice do most of their winter travelling this way, down where it's warm and sheltered and where their predators can't see them."

Jodie sighed. Outsmarting Grandma was tough. But then Jodie spotted a track even *she* was sure about. "Look, Grandma. Cow tracks."

Grandma looked — and shook her head. "Close, Jodie, but not quite. The cows can't get into this part of the pasture, remember? That's either a moose or an elk, probably heading for the field to steal a little hay."

Jodie gave up. She would *never* be as smart about animals as Grandma was. Now Grandma was pointing to another neat trail that headed off into the brush. "Here's one you can't go wrong on, Jodie."

"Don't count on it, Grandma. My batting average is pretty bad so far. Besides, those look just like cat tracks to me but I know they're not so there must be some wild animal that makes tracks like a cat."

Grandma shrugged. "Look like cat tracks to me."

Jodie stared at Grandma in amazement. "Really? Way out here in the woods? You think The Prince came out here hunting?"

"Well," Grandma laughed. "I guess it could be The Prince. But at this time of year I think he does most of his hunting out of a tin can."

Jodie laughed, too, thinking of the lazy, luxurious, longhaired Prince lying cozily on the couch with all four feet in the air. "Well, it sure wasn't Timothy T.," she said, giggling again at the thought. Fat, seventeen-year-old Timothy was enjoying his retirement in a box beside the fire. He got up only for breakfast, dinner, lunch, and tea — and assorted snacks in between.

"Could be a stray just living wild off the land," Grandma said.

"Can a cat get along without a home?"

"In the summer a good hunter could do just fine."

"But what about the winter?"

"Well, that depends on the winter. Weather like this, a little snow and not too cold, wouldn't bother a cat much."

"But what if it got forty below?" Jodie asked, remembering a bad cold spell last winter.

"Be pretty tough," Grandma admitted.

"Look," she added quickly, "there's a ruffed grouse's track."

But Jodie always knew when Grandma was trying to change the subject. She was not about to be shaken off. "Would the cat freeze out here, Grandma?" she asked.

Grandma breathed a deep sigh. "It might, Jodie," she said softly.

Suddenly the bright, sparkling, white and blue winter day seemed a little colder and the world seemed a sadder place. "It's not fair, Grandma," Jodie said, softly. "Just because he doesn't belong to somebody it's not fair he should just die out here when it gets cold."

Grandma put her arm around Jodie's shoulders and hugged her tight. "Jodie, darlin'," she said gently, "life isn't fair. It isn't fair to animals and it isn't fair to people. Learning that is one of the lessons of growing up."

Jodie looked up into Grandma's faded blue eyes and swallowed hard. "If that's what growing up is about, I don't think I want to do it."

Grandma smiled. "Some things we don't

get choices about. Look, there are the cows. They're still rustling some pretty good grass out from under the snow. As long as they can work for a living we won't have to start feeding . . ."

"Look at that!" Jodie interrupted, pointing past the grazing cattle to where a long line of huge, coffee-with-cream-coloured elk were making their way majestically across the field. "Aren't they beautiful?"

"They sure are, Jodie. Let's backtrack on their trail and find their bedground."

They found the place in a patch of poplars where the herd of elk had spent the night, packing the snow down into comfortable sleeping spots. Walking on, they also found a squirrel's pantry where he had been digging out his buried cones and having a winter snack. The winter woods were full of a hundred exciting surprises. Jodie didn't think any more about the homeless cat right then. But when she said her prayers that night, and every night afterward, she remembered to add, "And please look after the little cat who lives in the woods."

Time passed. Winter settled in. The snow

got deeper. Too deep for the cows to rustle through it to find the grass underneath. Every day Grandpa fired up either the truck or the tractor and took a big, round bale of hay out to feed them.

One cold evening after supper Grandpa looked up from the magazine he was reading. "Need a little exercise, Jodie-kid?" he asked.

Jodie felt a chore coming on. "Doing what?" she asked cautiously.

"It's going to be a cold one tonight and I forgot to plug the tractor in. You want to run over and do it for me?"

Jodie grinned. *That* wasn't much of a chore. "Sure, Grandpa." She grabbed her flashlight and jacket. "Come on, Miss Dog, let's go." Miss Dog eagerly jumped to her feet and together they headed into the cold, crisp night.

Over in the barnyard, Jodie pushed open the door to the tractor shed and swung the flashlight's beam around the dark interior. It was kind of spooky here at night, all silence and shadows. Suddenly, Jodie thought she saw something. A movement.

A flash of tawny grey. Then it was gone. What had she seen? Or had she seen anything at all? Maybe her eyes were playing tricks on her. She gave her head a shake and turned to consult her companion. "Miss Dog? Did you see something just then?"

Miss Dog cocked her head to one side, wagged vigorously, and grinned a large dog grin. Then she gave a low bark. Jodie sighed. "Miss Dog, either you'll have to learn English or I'll have to learn dog. I didn't understand a thing you just said." She plugged the tractor in and gave the flashlight one more slow sweep around the shed. Nothing moved. Jodie and Miss Dog went home.

A week passed. The days were getting short now. So short that it was growing dark when late-afternoon chore time rolled around. Both Grandma and Grandpa came down with a nasty case of the flu that week. Jodie insisted they both stay in and keep warm by the fire while she did afternoon chores. There wasn't much to do. Just make sure the water-tank heater was going and then drag a square bale of hay out of the tractor shed for the bulls' supper.

It was so dark in the shed that Jodie needed the flashlight again. (Grandpa kept saying he really *must* get an electric light put in there but Grandpa had a way of putting things off for a year or three.) She propped the light up on the floor, aimed at the bale stack, so she had both hands free. Then she climbed up to the top and pushed a bale off the edge. It hit the cement floor with a thud. And in that same second something that had been hiding behind the bale shot out of there like a bullet, hit the floor with a smaller thud, and went rocketing out the door and into the night so fast Jodie wondered if she'd seen it at all.

But she *had* seen it. It had glowing green eyes, a grey-tawny coat, and it looked a whole lot like a cat to her. She didn't say anything to Grandma and Grandpa yet, but she decided a little scientific experiment wouldn't hurt.

Next day she brought a dish of dry cat food out and hid it behind a bale on top of the stack. When she checked the dish the following day it was polished cleaner than Grandma's best china. Yes, thought Jodie, if it *looks* like a cat, and it *eats* like a cat, it must *be* a cat. And I intend to *meet* that cat. She filled the dish again.

Right after supper that night Jodie took a stroll out to the shed. "You wait out here," she whispered to a disappointed Miss Dog as she opened the door and quietly slipped inside. Slowly she shone the flashlight beam around the shed. There it was! A flash of green. Jodie moved the light back again. From the top of the bale stack two green eyes peered cautiously down at her. Two green eyes attached to a compact little tawny-grey and black pin-striped body. A cat with one thin black stripe that ran right around her throat like a delicate necklace. "Katie the Kitty," Jodie whispered, her memory taking her back to her favourite picture book when she was little.

Katie didn't move. She just sat there, very alert, her ears at attention and her eyes on Jodie. "Don't be afraid, little Katie," Jodie whispered, "I won't hurt you." She took one slow, cautious step forward. Katie still didn't move. Talking softly all the way, Jodie took another step, and another. Now she was at the base of the bale pile. Slowly, ever so slowly, she reached a hand up toward the cat. Still, Katie held her ground. Jodie stopped short of actually touching her. She just held her hand there, a whisker's-length from the cat's face.

For a long minute Katie sat unmoving, staring down at her. Then, all of a sudden, she made up her mind. With a soft "Murrp!" she stretched out her neck and rubbed her cheek against Jodie's hand. Jodie gave her a gentle fingertip scratch right in the itchy spot beneath her ear where all cats love to be rubbed. Katie squinched up her green eyes with pleasure. Somewhere inside her a small motor began to run. And in that moment Jodie knew that Katie had become her cat.

After a few moments of petting, Katie jumped lightly to the floor for a closer inspection of Jodie. After more visiting and another cat food snack, Katie walked over to the small opening where the big sliding doors didn't quite meet. She stuck her nose out and sniffed the air. Quickly she jerked her head back inside, shook her whiskers, and sneezed. Then she came back to Jodie, gave her ankles a friendly rub, and looked up into her face. "Meow?" she said in a questioning tone.

Jodie laughed. "Yeah, Katie, it *is* cold out there tonight. You want to know if you can move in here permanently, don't you?" Katie smiled a cat smile. Jodie gave her a rub behind the ears. "Welcome home, Katie Cat."

Jodie broke the news to Grandma and Grandpa about the new member of the family. Grandpa grumbled about "critters eating him out of house and home." Then he grinned and rumpled Jodie's hair and Jodie knew he didn't mind. Grandma looked a little more thoughtful. "I suppose it's a female," she said, not too enthusiastically. It occurred to Jodie that she really had no idea whether it was a male or a female.

"I don't know, Grandma," she said. "It just looked like a Katie-cat to me so that's what I called it."

"It'll be a female," Grandma declared. "And before spring she's going to the vet for a little operation or we'll have a whole batch of cats before we know what hit us. I'm not about to have a whole barnful of starving cats we can't afford to feed."

"Okay, Grandma. I'll even help pay the vet from my allowance."

The winter stretched out, long and cold and hard. But no matter how cold the day, when Jodie walked out into the barnyard the little cat with the thin black necklace always came out to meet her. Katie was very happy to be Jodie's cat, she said in loud purrs every time they met.

Calving time came. Things got very busy around the ranch. The last thing on anyone's mind was one small barn cat who really ought to go see the vet. Then Grandma's arthritis acted up for a whole month and she hardly got out to the barnyard. She was so disgusted about being stuck in the house that she forgot that spring was just around the corner.

Meanwhile, little Katie, the stray, had done very well for herself. She was a full-grown cat now — big, sleek, and downright fat. Maybe it was time to cut back on the cat food a little, Jodie thought. She tried, but

Katie complained loudly. She was *very* hungry these days. A suspicion began to creep into Jodie's mind, but she buried it in a back corner and refused to think about it — most of the time. When it did sneak into her thoughts it always came with a question. What will Grandma say?

And then one beautiful day in late May, Katie disappeared. When she didn't show up for breakfast, Jodie thought she was on a hunting trip. When she didn't come for supper, Jodie didn't know what to think. She called and called and called. Once she thought she heard a very soft answering meow somewhere deep in the maze of the bale stack. But when Jodie called again there was no answer at all. Maybe the meow had been just wishful thinking. That night, Katie had an important place in Jodie's prayers again.

The next morning Jodie walked slowly to the barnyard. She was almost afraid to look in the shed in case she saw a lot of emptiness where her Katie-cat should be. She took a deep breath and opened the door. There was no cat in sight. Jodie swallowed hard. Then, something caught her eye. Katie's dish. Jodie had left it filled last night, just in case. Now it was empty and polished so clean it shone.

"Katie?" Jodie half whispered the word, almost afraid to believe.

"Murrup!" It was the happiest cat-sound Jodie had ever heard. Katie was smiling a cat-smile all over her whiskers as she came bounding out from behind a bale and landed next to Jodie. Katie had never looked so good: bright-eyed and bushy tailed, sleek and well-groomed — and much slimmer than she had been for a long time. "Oh, Katie! What have you gone and done?" whispered Jodie as she bent to stroke the cat's silky head.

Katie just smiled and purred and said she was *very* hungry.

While Katie ate her breakfast, Jodie did some detective work. She backtracked from where Katie had appeared, carefully checking each space and hollow between the bales. Suddenly, she thought she heard a tiny sound. She froze, staring into the shadowy dimness of a little hay cave beneath an overhanging bale. Something moved in there. Jodie reached in with a cautious hand and touched — the softest something she had ever felt. Something soft and warm, and very much alive. She moved her hand around. There were four somethings. Jodie *had* to see. Very slowly, making sure not to scare them, she crawled back out of the bale tunnel. Once out she began to run as fast as she could back to the house.

She whirled in through the back door like a tornado, grabbed the flashlight, and was halfway out again when Grandma stopped her. "Jodie Anne McCrimmon! What on *earth* has gotten into you?"

"I, um, I'm exploring, Grandma! I need the flashlight." She flew out the door and back to the barnyard.

Shining the light ahead of her, Jodie crept quietly into the dim hay tunnel. The light caught a glow of green. Two watchful eyes looking up at Jodie. Katie had returned to her cozy nest. "Hi, Katie," Jodie said softly. "Don't worry. I just want to look." Katie gave a soft, friendly "Murrp" that sounded like she would be very pleased for Jodie to have a look.

Jodie gave Katie a gentle scratch behind her ears. Then she focused the light down into the hay beside Katie. There, cuddled close beside her, were four tiny, perfect, squirming bits of fur. Kittens so tiny Jodie could have held all four in the palm of her hand. "Oh, Katie," Jodie said in a hushed voice, "they're so beautiful!"

They came in matched pairs, like mittens. Two were like their mother, tabbies with fine pin stripes all through their suits. One was dark, the other lighter, more the colour of Katie. The other two were also tabby-coloured, but their stripes were wide and bold. Those two must have inherited their father's coat, Jodie decided. "Katie," she asked thoughtfully, giving the cat another rub behind the ears, "did you marry an escaped convict with stripes like that in his suit?" Katie just purred a little louder and smiled a cat smile.

Jodie studied the kittens one by one. The dark pin-striped one looked like a woods trail in fall when sunlight fell in narrow strips between thin, leafless poplar trees, leaving the spaces between in dark bands of shadow. "Shadow," Jodie announced. "That's going to be your name."

She looked at the lighter-coloured pin-striped kitten, practically identical to its mother, just one shade greyer. "Little Katie," she decided. (It had better be a girl or it would go through life a very embarrassed cat!)

Then she turned to the bold-striped kittens. One had a white vest and four dazzling white socks. "Sox," she announced, mentally spelling it with an "x." She *liked* sox spelled that way, but her teacher always corrected it in her stories. No way could she correct *this* one! The last kitten was the smallest of all — so small that its huge dark stripes almost overwhelmed it. "You're nothing but a little zebra!" Jodie exclaimed, and then Zeb had a name, too.

Suddenly Jodie got a "being-watched" feeling. She glanced over her shoulder. "Grandma!"

"I thought something was going on out here," Grandma said.

"Oh, Grandma, did you see them? They're so beautiful."

Grandma nodded solemnly. "Yes, all four of them. Five barn cats plus two house cats makes too many cats, Jodie," she said in a tired voice. "You can pick two of the kittens to keep and the other two we'll have put to sleep right away before they get their eyes open."

Jodie could hardly believe her ears. "But, Grandma . . ." she said, her voice barely above a whisper.

Grandma shook her head. "I'm sorry Jodie. We should have taken Katie to the vet long ago. But now that the kittens are here we just can't keep them all."

Jodie turned back to look at the four tiny, sleeping bundles of fur.

"Choose two," Grandma said.

Jodie stared at the kittens until her eyes began to blur. The tears were starting down her cheeks as she turned to Grandma again. "I *can't* choose," she whispered. "It's just not fair to say, 'you two live and you two die.'" She started to squeeze past Grandma, to get out of there so she didn't have to look at two doomed kittens any more.

But as she brushed against her arm, Grandma reached out to stop her. Jodie looked up into Grandma's face. To her amazement, there were tears in Grandma's eyes, too. "I know you can't choose, Jodie, darlin'. Sitting here looking at them, I realized that I couldn't choose either. I guess the ranch is just going to *have* to support seven cats after all."

"Oh, Grandma, thank you!" Jodie flung her arms around Grandma's neck and squeezed with all her might. Grandma squeezed her back.

Then she broke free and gave Jodie a stern look. "But you can be sure of this, Jodie. The minute they're old enough, the *whole* family is going to the vet to get fixed so we don't get *another* crop of kittens. This is a *cattle* ranch, not a *cat* ranch, you know. And, what's more, young lady, your allowance is going to help pay for all those vet bills."

Jodie looked at her beautiful fur family and decided it would be the best money she ever spent.

Katie took one more long, thoughtful look at her humans and breathed a sigh that was half a purr. Then she fell asleep with her paws wrapped around her kittens.

OUTLAW MOUSE

Grandma and Grandpa were in the living room watching the news that cold winter evening. Jodie was at the kitchen table having milk and peanut butter cookies to help her finish her homework. As she glanced up from her book she thought she caught a movement in the shadows over by the fridge. She blinked and stared in that direction. Nothing.

"Eye strain from too much studying," she muttered to herself. "Someone should tell teachers that homework is hazardous to the health. Much more of this math and I'll have to borrow Grandpa's bifocals."

She leaned over her work. There it was again. Out of the corner of her eye she had *definitely* seen something move this time. Very slowly, she turned her head. And there it was. Sitting in front of the fridge as if it owned the kitchen. A tiny, sleek and shiny, brownish mouse with huge ears, bright eyes, and white trim around its edges. It was the most fascinating thing Jodie had ever seen in the kitchen. She opened her mouth to share the miracle with Grandma, but then she closed it again. Grandma was as much an animal lover as anyone Jodie knew, but a mouse in her kitchen might just be where she drew the line. Anyway, it would be kind of neat to have this for her own little secret.

Moving very slowly, Jodie broke a crumb off her cookie and tossed it over near the mouse. The mouse panicked and dived under the fridge. Jodie pretended to go back to her homework. A minute or two passed. Sure enough. Out came the mouse. He came in little rushes, pausing to check for danger, and then rushing forward again. He grabbed the crumb and, like lightning, was back under the fridge. Jodie smiled, thinking of the secret mouse picnic taking place right here in the kitchen.

For the next few days, Jodie kept an eye out for her mouse, but it was getting close to Christmas and Grandma bustled around the kitchen baking late into most evenings. The mouse must be playing it safe and staying hidden till everyone was in bed. In fact, he had stayed hidden so long that Jodie had almost forgotten about him — until she heard an early-morning squawk from Grandma.

The words "Good land! What's happened to my mince pie?" woke Jodie from a Saturday-morning sleep-in. She jumped out of bed and got to the kitchen in time to hear, "Harold! We've got a mouse! The little varmint has helped himself to the edge of my pie I left cooling on the counter overnight!"

Grandpa looked over the top of the cattle magazine he was reading while he waited for the breakfast coffee to heat. There was a mischievous twinkle in his eye. "Calm down now, Ellen," he drawled. "Little fella didn't eat *much*, did he?"

Jodie always suspected Grandpa had come dangerously close to receiving one almost-whole mince pie in the face at that moment. But Grandma controlled herself and sent him off to the basement to hunt for a mousetrap. Jodie crossed her fingers and wished that he wouldn't find one. It worked! Fifteen minutes later he came grumbling back upstairs with cobwebs in his hair and announced that there were no mousetraps in the basement.

Grandma muttered something about him not being able to find his hat if it was on his head and took matters into her own hands. It took more than crossed fingers to stop Grandma. Five minutes later she was back with two traps. "There!" she said to Grandpa with satisfaction, "*you* be sure to set them before we go to bed tonight."

Jodie glanced toward the shadowy space under the refrigerator. You'd better be listening, mouse! Get out of town before nightfall or the sheriff's gonna get you.

Bedtime came. Grandpa had a snack and

then headed off down the hall toward the bedroom. Grandma caught him. "Harold, the mousetrap. Here," she said, handing him a jar of peanut butter. "Bait it with this."

Grandpa stared at it. "What's this? You bait mouse traps with cheese."

Grandma shook her head. "You're behind the times, Harold. I read that mice love peanut butter."

"If you ask me, I'd say they love mince pie," Grandpa muttered.

Grandma shot him a stern look. "Just bait the trap, Harold."

Grandpa baited and set the traps. He put one on the counter and one by the basement door. He probably should have put one beside the refrigerator, Jodie thought. But she kept her thoughts to herself.

Everyone went to bed. That included Timothy T., the senior citizen cat, who went to his cozy box on the porch and Prince, the handsome tabby, who slept with Jodie. Before the cats went, Grandma gave them both a stern talking-to about neglecting their work. They yawned.

Jodie spent a restless night. She kept

waking up and lying listening, hoping not to hear a sudden sharp *snap!* from the kitchen. Finally she slept soundly, only to wake before seven and lie there wondering what she was worrying about.

Suddenly she remembered. Her mouse! She had to know the awful truth. She threw on her robe and rushed to the kitchen. Both traps were mercifully mouse-free. Jodie let out a huge sigh of relief. Then she took a closer look. Both traps were peanut-butter-free, too. Every morsel had been polished off, leaving the trap as clean as a new-washed plate. Jodie giggled. Oh mouse, you're a slick one!

Grandma was not in the least amused when *she* saw the empty traps. That evening she coached Grandpa as he reset the traps. "Now, adjust the trigger a little finer this time, Harold. Last time you set it so that mouse could nibble all the peanut butter off without setting off the spring. No, Harold, you've still not set it fine enough. Just move that trigger a little more, just a bit . . ."

Snap! Grandpa let out a roar like a wounded buffalo as the mouse trap went off, trapping him by the little finger. Gingerly, he released it and stood blowing cool air on his stinging pinky.

"Whoops!" Grandma said in a small voice.

Grandpa placed the unset trap firmly in Grandma's hand. "Goodnight, Ellen," he said and marched off to bed.

That night, Grandma set the traps. Jodie noticed that she didn't push *her* luck making too fine a trigger adjustment.

The next morning the peanut butter was gone again. Jodie grinned to herself. The score was Mouse 2, Grandma 0.

Christmas was getting close. Grandma got busier and busier. The next night Jodie noticed that nobody set the mousetraps. She breathed a sigh of relief and had a wonderful night's sleep.

The subject of the mouse didn't come up again for several days, although Jodie did notice that Grandma no longer left her baking to cool on the counter overnight. Maybe the mouse had taken Jodie's advice and moved out of the house. Or maybe one of the cats had caught him for a midnight snack while everyone was sleeping. Somehow, Jodie doubted that had happened. The cats seemed hungrier than usual. Every morning the dish of Cat Chow left out for them overnight had been completely devoured.

Jodie finished her Christmas shopping. Almost, that is. She had a fantastic jackknife for Grandpa, a Toronto Blue Jays cap for her friend, Eric, but she was having trouble getting just the right thing for Grandma. She had bought her a pretty scarf but she still had a little money left and was trying to think of some little gift that would be just what Grandma really needed.

Christmas came closer. Jodie started wrapping presents. She needed a red bow to top off Eric's gift. She thought she remembered Grandma putting some bows into the sewing-machine drawer awhile ago. She went searching. Yes, there was a red bow in there. But — but, it was almost buried! For a minute Jodie just stood staring with her mouth wide open. "Gra . . ." she began but then she shut her mouth. This was not something Grandma needed to hear about right now. The drawer was nearly filled with Cat

Chow! And Jodie had a very good idea about whose secret storehouse this must be. What a sassy mouse! Stealing from the cats! The little guy had nerve, all right. Very quietly Jodie scooped up the kidnapped cat food and put it back into the cats' dish.

When suppertime came around, the cats trooped out to their dish. They sniffed it and twitched their whiskers and stood staring with very odd expressions on their faces. "Hmmph!" Grandma said. "Those cats are getting awfully high and mighty. They act like they smell a rat in their cat food." Jodie didn't say a word.

It was now only two days before Christmas. Time for the Christmas tree hunt when Jodie and Grandma and Grandpa would walk far back into the deep woods to find the perfect spruce. The snow was deep and it was cold out. Grandma decided her rubber boots wouldn't do. She would have to dig her cozy, fleece-lined lace-up boots out of the depths of the back closet. She found them and dragged them out of the shadowy closet. She started to put her foot into one. Suddenly she stopped. "What on earth?"

She flicked on the light to find out why she couldn't get her foot into her boot.

Jodie looked up from reading Jenkins' Hardware Christmas sale catalogue and rushed out to see what was going on. She and Grandma stood in silent amazement. Both of Grandma's winter boots were filled to the brim with Cat Chow! It reminded Jodie of when they had studied "Christmas in Other Lands" at school last year. In some countries kids didn't put out their stockings for Santa to fill. They put out their shoes instead. "Merry Christmas, Grandma!" Jodie giggled.

"That does it!" Grandma declared. "That mouse has gone too far. Right after Christmas I'm going to buy half a dozen new traps and declare war." Then, in spite of herself she began to grin. "Little varmint *does* have a sense of humour, though, doesn't he?"

Right then something clicked in Jodie's head. Something she had seen in the catalogue. Suddenly, she knew what Grandma's *really* special Christmas present was going to be.

The next day when Grandma went to

town to mail some last-minute cards, Jodie went along. "I'll only be a minute, Grandma!" she called over her shoulder. Then she ran all the way to Jenkins' Hardware Store. Mrs. Jenkins had exactly what she needed. She even wrapped it up in Christmas paper and put on a red bow — one that *hadn't* been buried in Cat Chow.

It was Christmas Eve. Grandma invited Eric's family over for hot chocolate and cookies. Jodie gave Eric his cap. Eric gave her one of the Black Stallion books that she was collecting. By the time they had left it was getting late. "Into bed, Jodie-kid," Grandpa ordered. "Santa Claus won't come if you're still awake," he added with a wink.

"Okay, Grandpa," Jodie said with a big yawn. Then she thought of something. "Grandma, I want you to open part of your present tonight so you can try it out right away."

Grandma looked very puzzled. "Hmm. Must be a nightgown in that case. The only thing I plan to do yet today is crawl into bed."

Jodie giggled and handed over the square present with the bow on top. Grandma shook it. It gave sort of a muffled rattle. She squeezed it. It was hard as steel. "Open it, Grandma!" Grandma opened it. Inside was a square steel box with a little square opening on each end and a hinged lid that opened.

Grandma looked at it. She turned it upside down and looked at it. Finally she shrugged. "It's, uh, a very pretty metal box, Jodie. What, uh, do I do with it?"

Jodie laughed. "You use it to get your kitchen back, Grandma! It's a live mousetrap. See, there's a little teeter-totter thing inside. The mouse can walk up the little ramp but when he tries to walk back out it shifts and doesn't leave him room to get out the door. Mrs. Jenkins says it's guaranteed to work and it doesn't hurt the mouse one bit."

Grandma shook her head. "Well, now I've seen everything. But, I'll bet you no self-respecting mouse is dumb enough to just march right in there."

"Bet he is," Jodie said, "especially for

this." She took the last bite of the mince tart she'd been eating and pushed it inside the trap. "Why don't you set it up, uh, right in front of the refrigerator?"

Grandma set the trap on the floor. With one last suspicious glance over her shoulder, she went off to bed. Jodie gave the trap one last glance, too, crossed her fingers, and also went to bed.

Sleeping on Christmas Eve was never easy. It took Jodie a long time to settle down, but finally she drifted off to dream of a jolly fat man landing on her roof.

Suddenly, she woke up. She had just heard the strangest noise. For a minute there she thought she really was hearing tiny hooves scratching and pawing on her roof. Whoa, Jodie! she thought. You really *are* a little beyond that stuff. Anyway, this was sort of a scratching-on-metal sound. It came again. Not from the roof, but from the kitchen. Jodie crawled out of bed and went to investigate.

The sound was coming from the refrigerator. No, from in front of the refrigerator. From inside the box in front of the refrigerator.

Carefully Jodie picked up the mousetrap and peered in through an airhole. A beady black eye peered right back at her. Outlaw Mouse had been captured.

Before the family could open any presents Christmas morning they had a job to do. Outlaw Mouse was going straight — straight outside where mice belong. Grandpa scouted out a spot. A huge fallen tree with lots of nice dry grass underneath for a mouse to make a cozy nest. Jodie carried the metal box with the prisoner inside. Grandma said to go ahead, she'd be along in a minute. When she caught up Jodie was just ready to open the lid of the trap and release the mouse.

"Ready, Grandma?" she asked. Grandma nodded. Jodie opened the trap. For a minute the mouse sat frozen, his whiskers twitching as he took in his new surroundings. Then he shot out of the box and dived into the deep grass under the fallen tree.

That's when Grandma brought the remains of her ruined mince pie out from behind her back. "I've had it in the freezer ever since he nibbled it," she said with a

sheepish smile. "I knew I'd find a use for it."
She set it down on the ground under the
tree.

"Merry Christmas, mouse!"